MONKEY & ROBOT

Friends and Neighbors

Peter Catalanotto

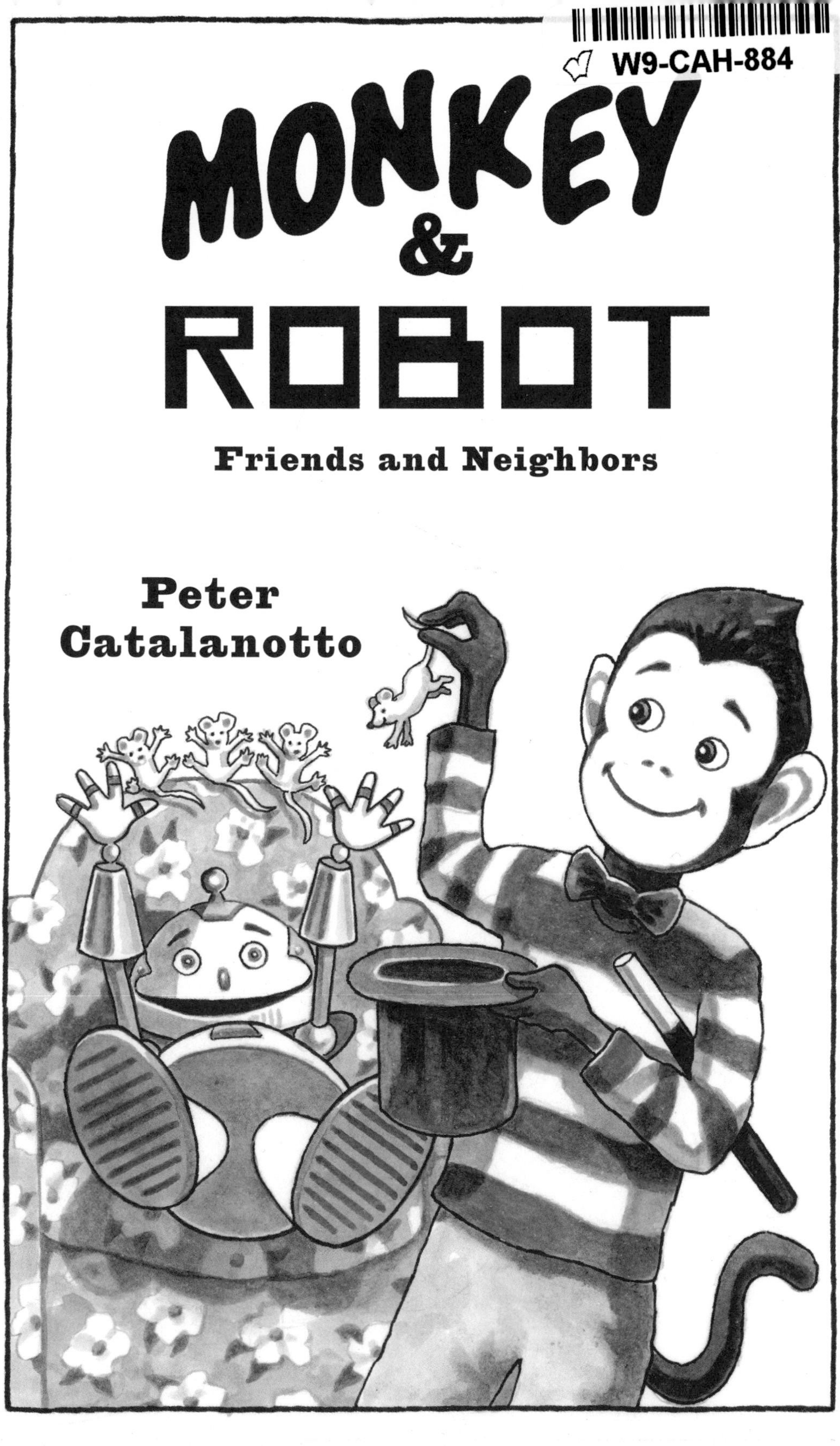

To Sarah, for whose wondrous heart I am grateful every day.

Special thanks to Marissa and Simon.

Copyright © 2019 Peter Catalanotto
Cover and internal design by Simon Stahl

MIX
Paper from
responsible sources
FSC® C016973

CIP data for this book is available from the Library of Congress.

Published by Creston Books, LLC
www.crestonbooks.co

ISBN 978-1-939547-59-0
Source of Production: 1010 Printing
Printed and bound in China
5 4 3 2 1

Creston Books

Contents

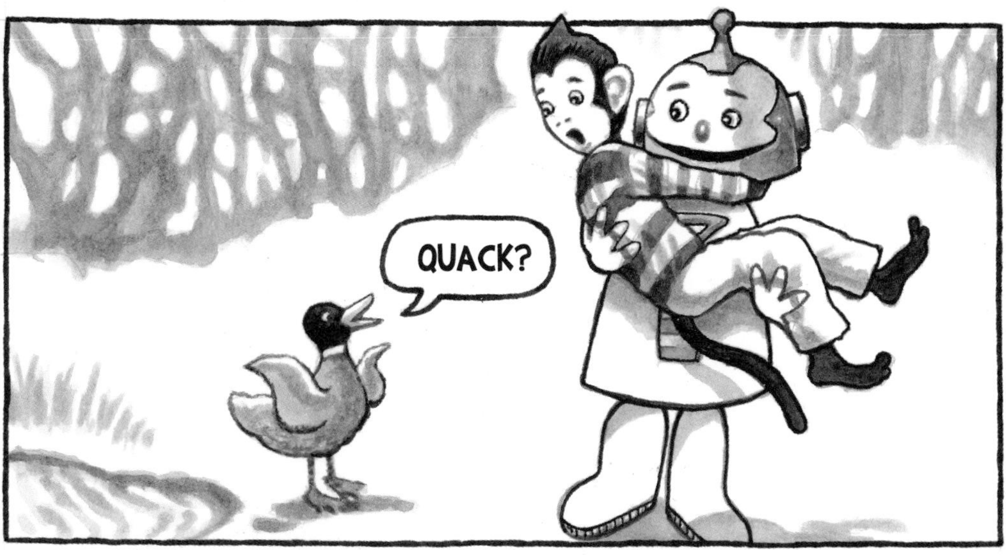

QUACK?

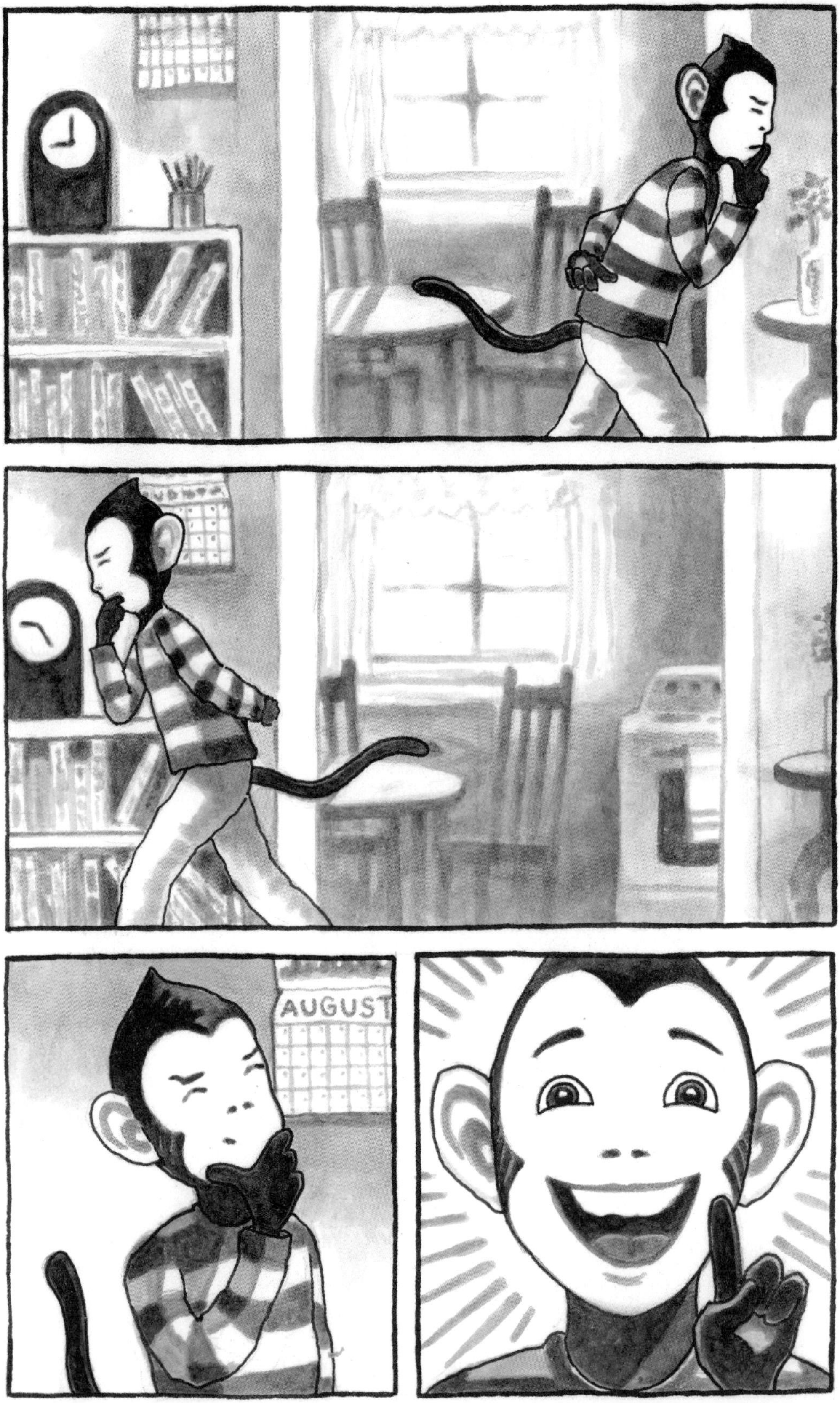
AUGUST

Happy Built-Day!

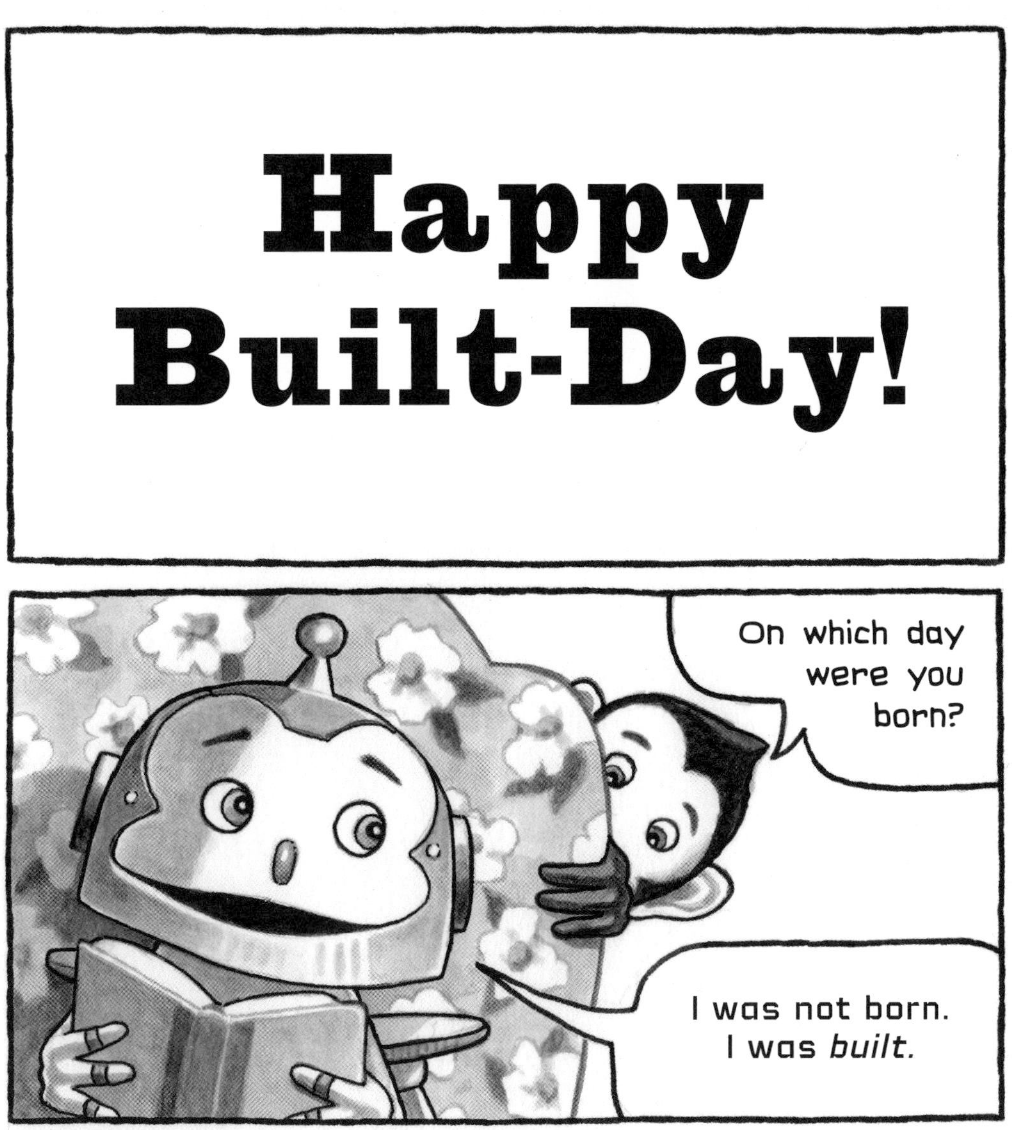
On which day were you born?
I was not born. I was *built.*

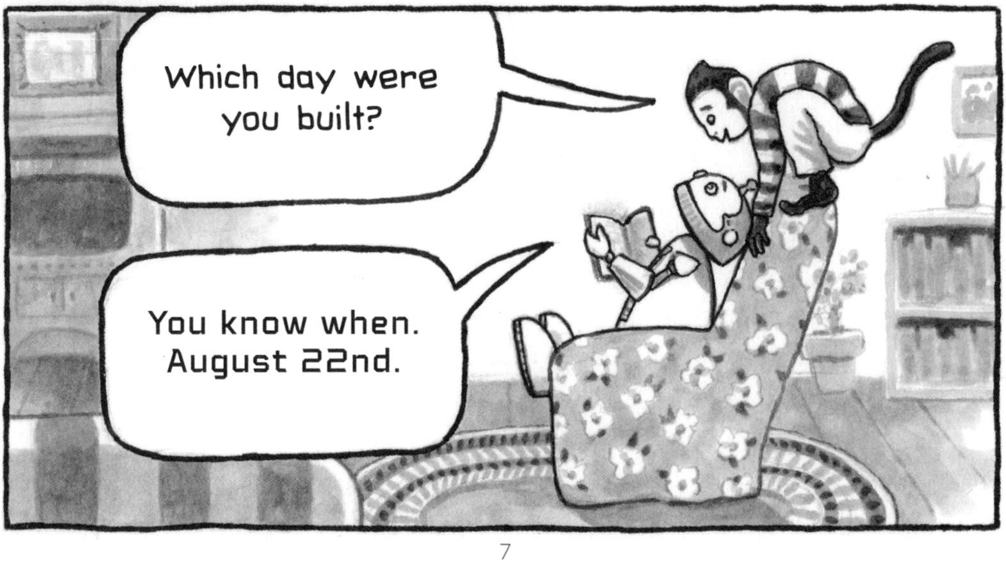
Which day were you built?
You know when. August 22nd.

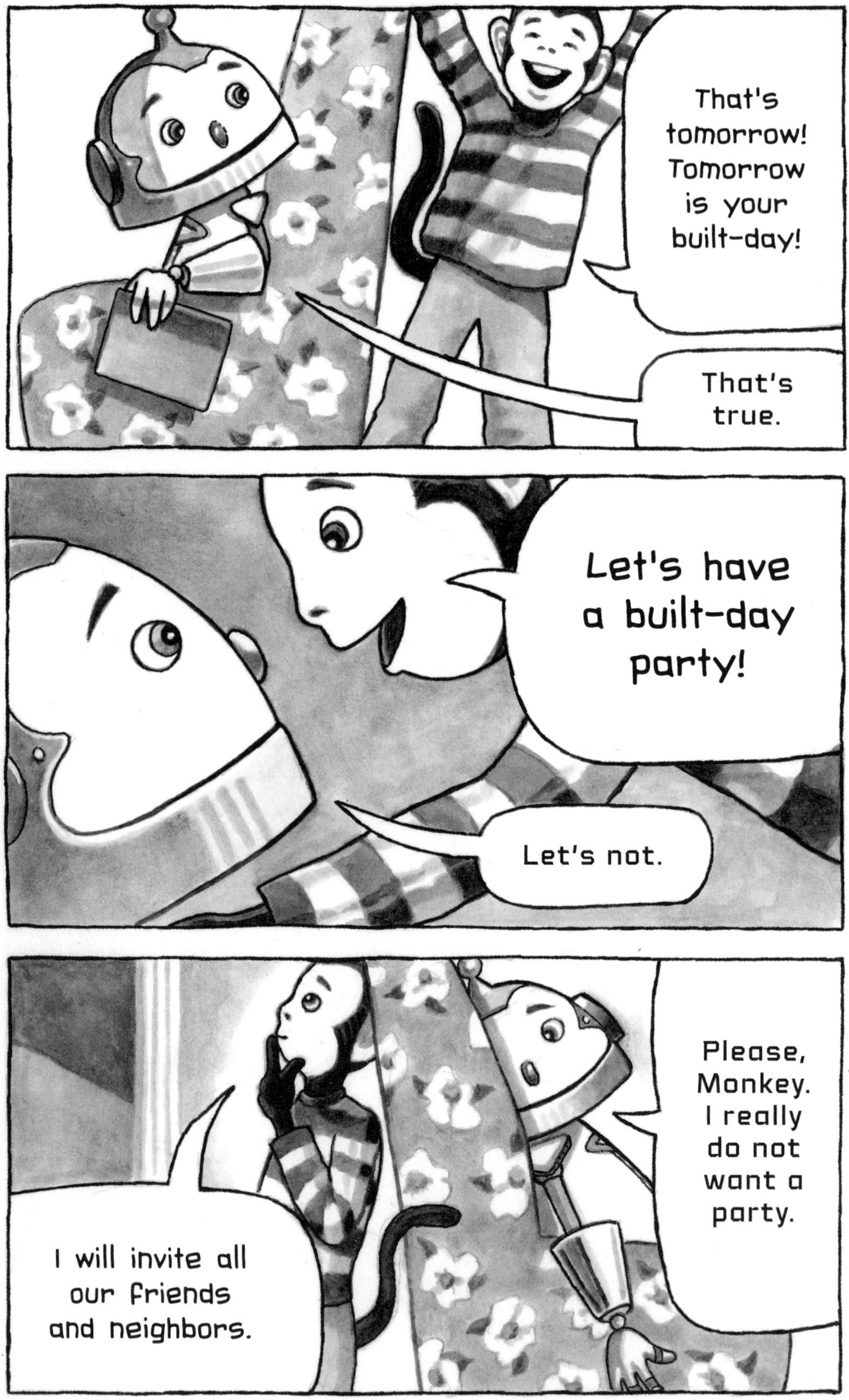
That's tomorrow! Tomorrow is your built-day!
That's true.
Let's have a built-day party!
Let's not.
Please, Monkey. I really do not want a party.
I will invite all our friends and neighbors.

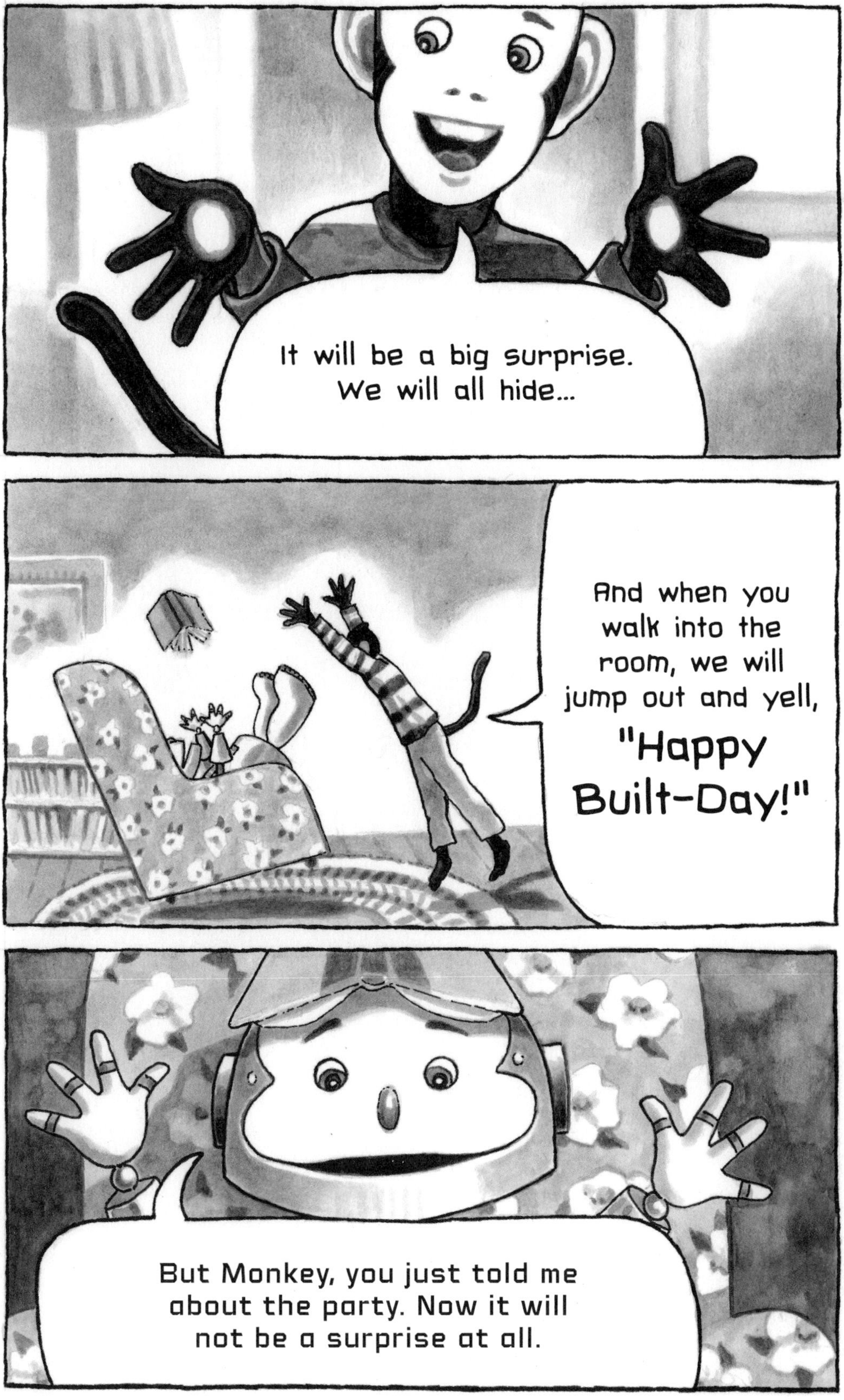
It will be a big surprise. We will all hide...
And when you walk into the room, we will jump out and yell, "Happy Built-Day!"
But Monkey, you just told me about the party. Now it will not be a surprise at all.

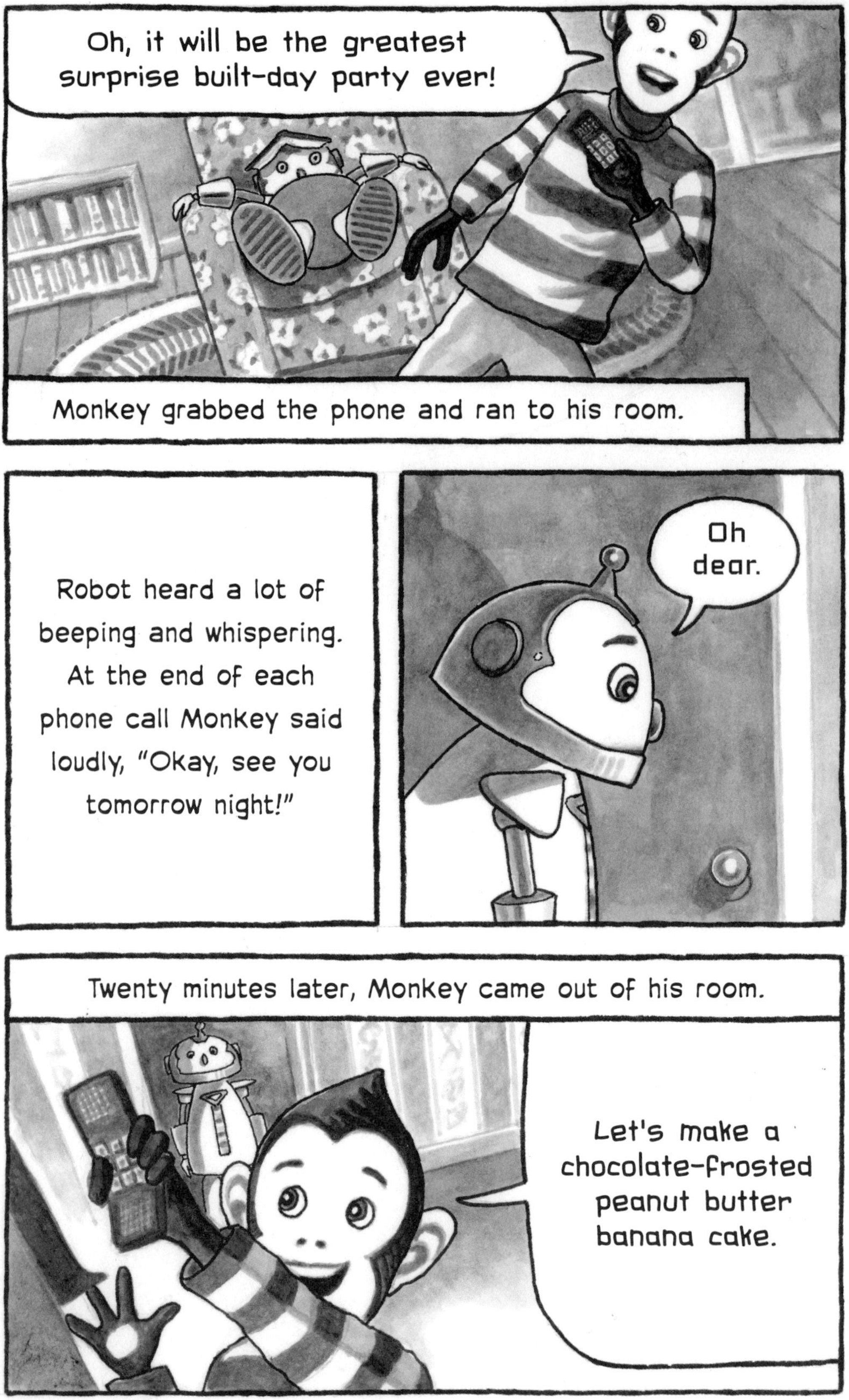
Oh, it will be the greatest surprise built-day party ever!
Monkey grabbed the phone and ran to his room.
Robot heard a lot of beeping and whispering. At the end of each phone call Monkey said loudly, "Okay, see you tomorrow night!"
Oh dear.
Twenty minutes later, Monkey came out of his room.
Let's make a chocolate-frosted peanut butter banana cake.

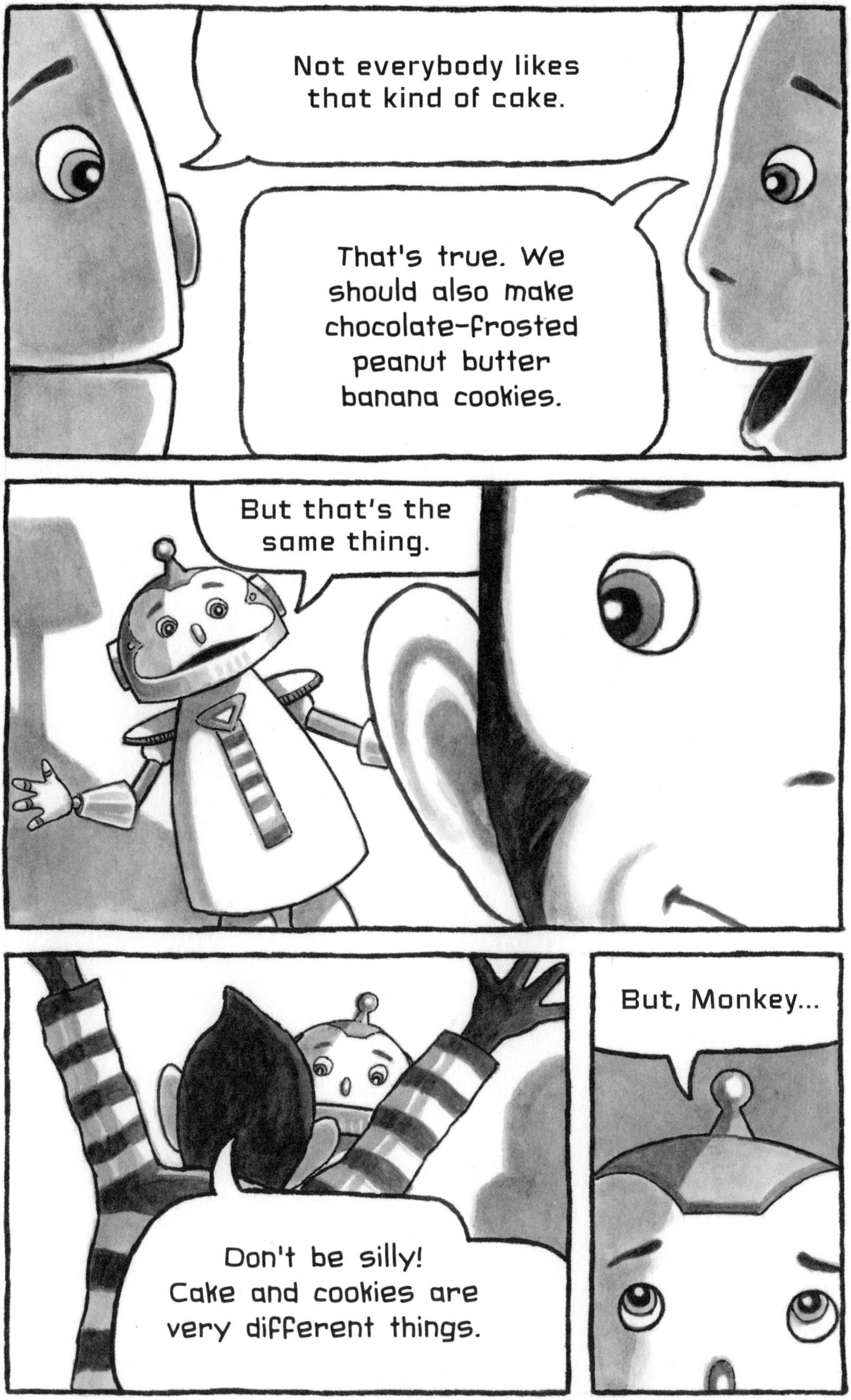
Not everybody likes that kind of cake.
That's true. We should also make chocolate-frosted peanut butter banana cookies.
But that's the same thing.
Don't be silly! Cake and cookies are very different things.
But, Monkey...

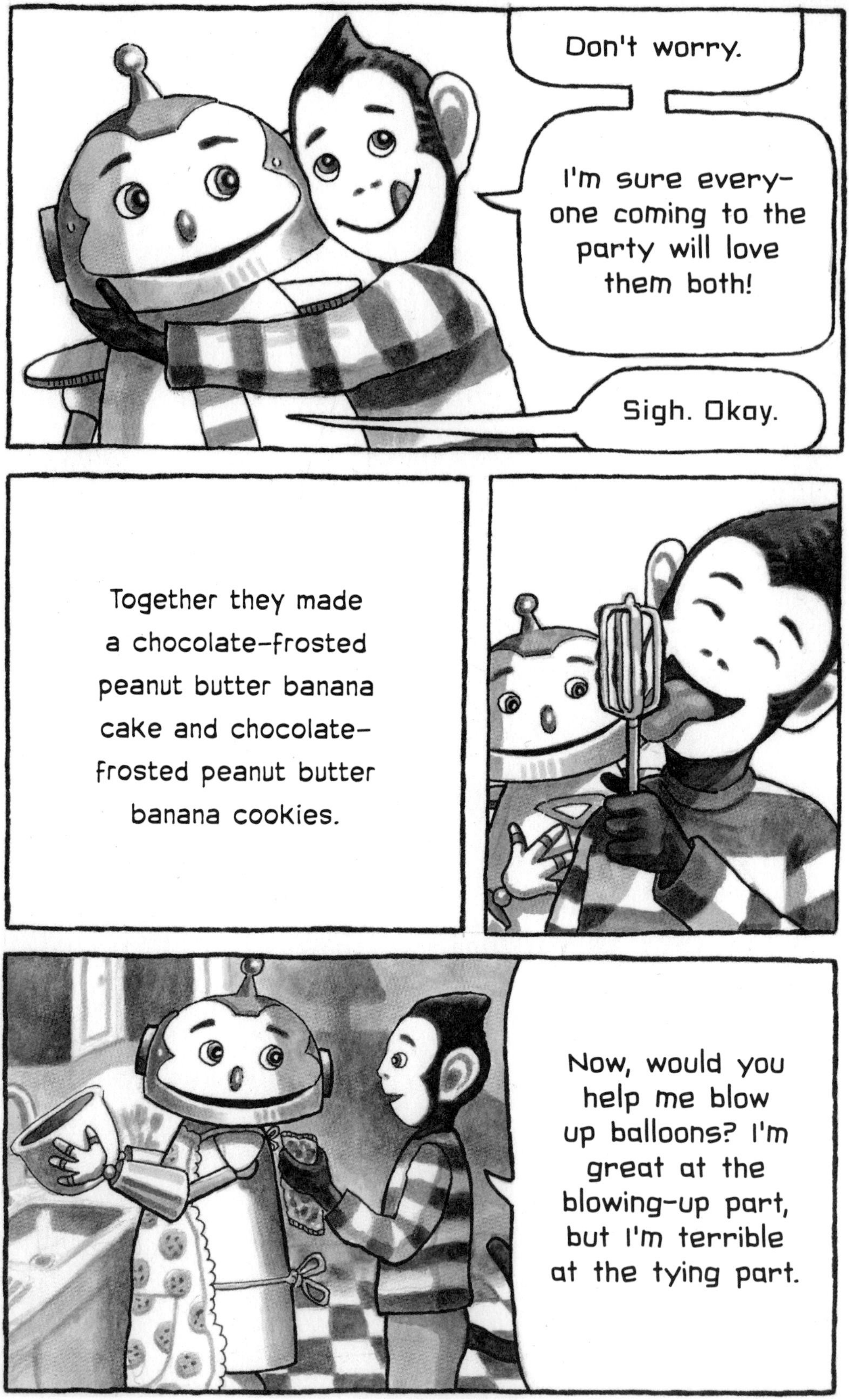
Don't worry.
I'm sure every-one coming to the party will love them both!
Sigh. Okay.
Together they made a chocolate-frosted peanut butter banana cake and chocolate-frosted peanut butter banana cookies.
Now, would you help me blow up balloons? I'm great at the blowing-up part, but I'm terrible at the tying part.

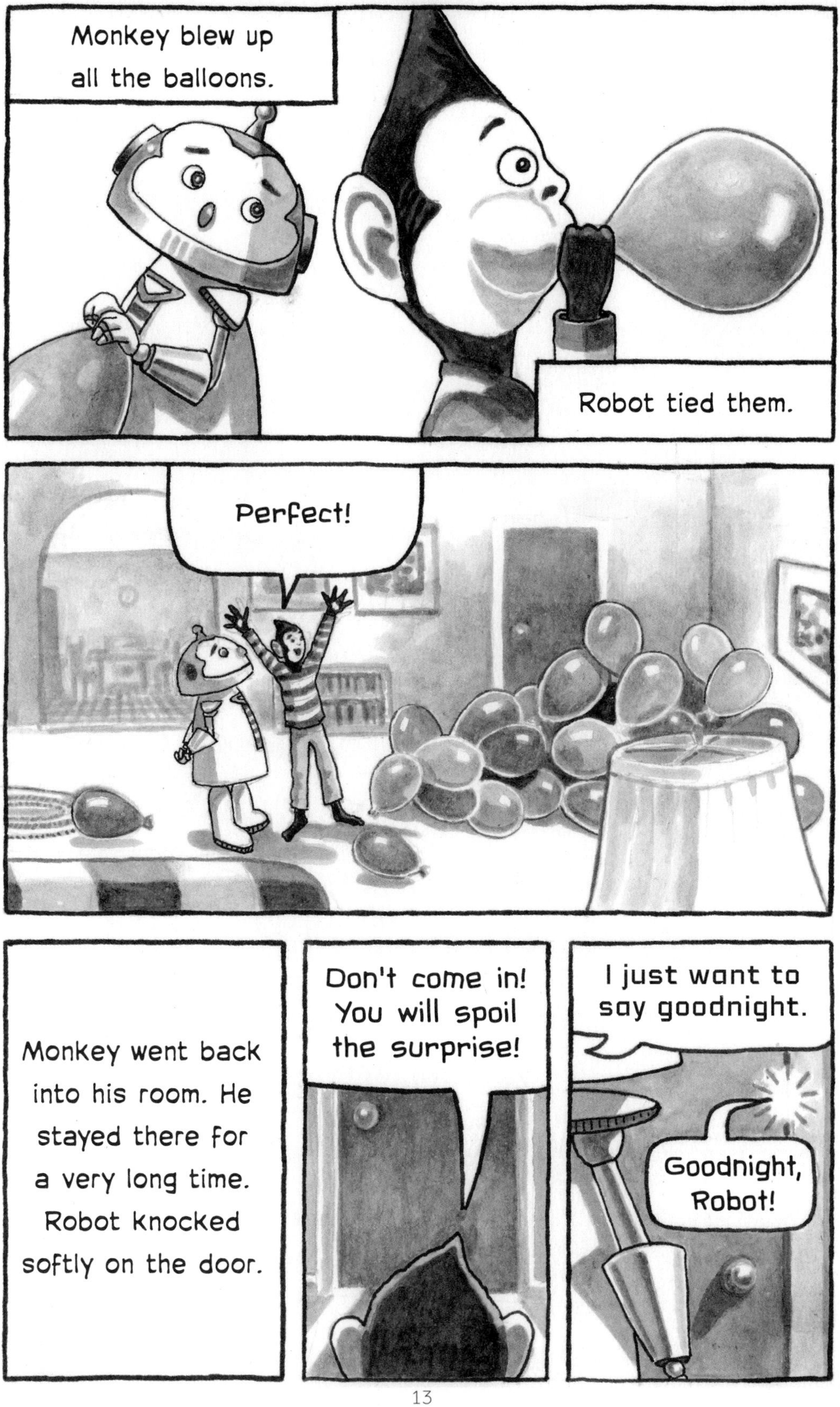
Monkey blew up all the balloons.
Robot tied them.
Perfect!
Monkey went back into his room. He stayed there for a very long time. Robot knocked softly on the door.
Don't come in! You will spoil the surprise!
I just want to say goodnight.
Goodnight, Robot!

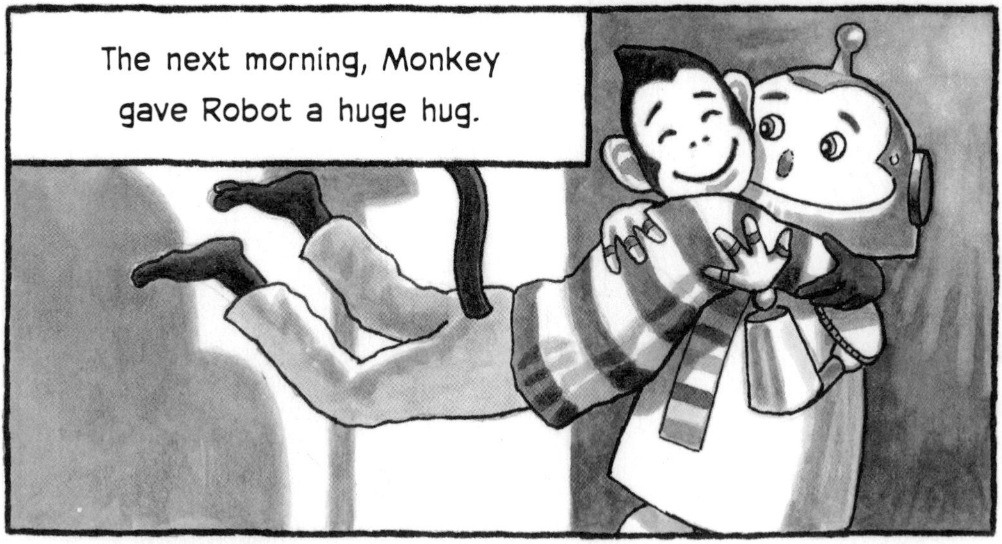
The next morning, Monkey gave Robot a huge hug.

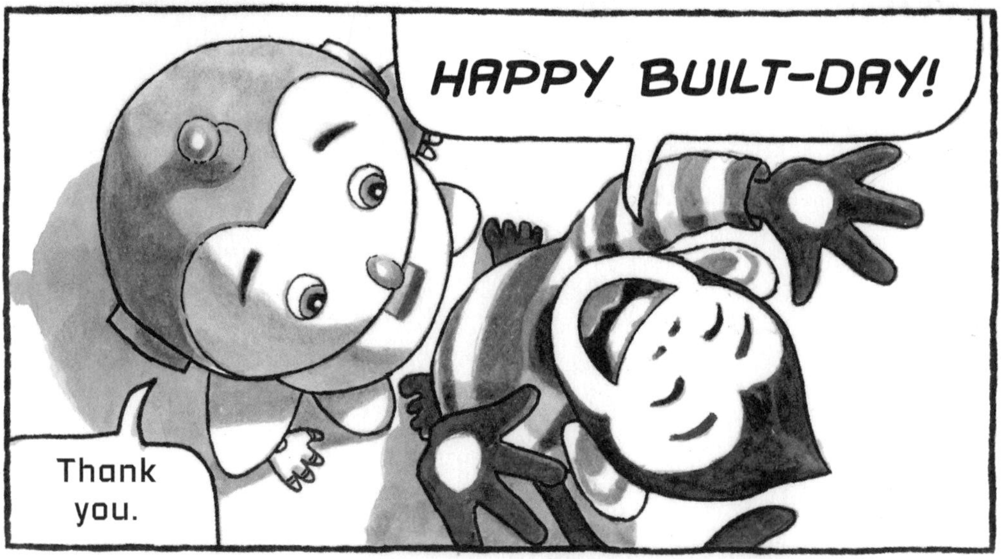
HAPPY BUILT-DAY!
Thank you.

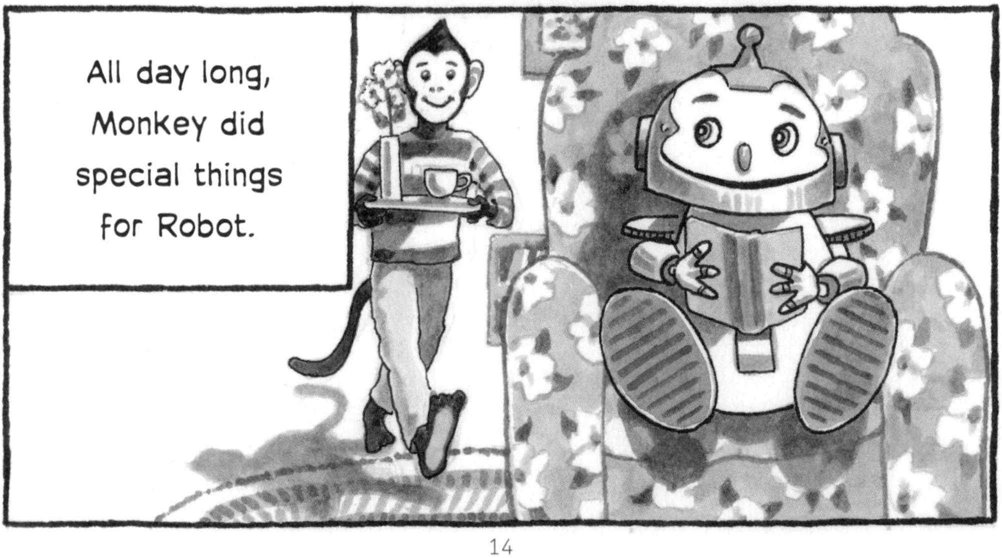
All day long, Monkey did special things for Robot.

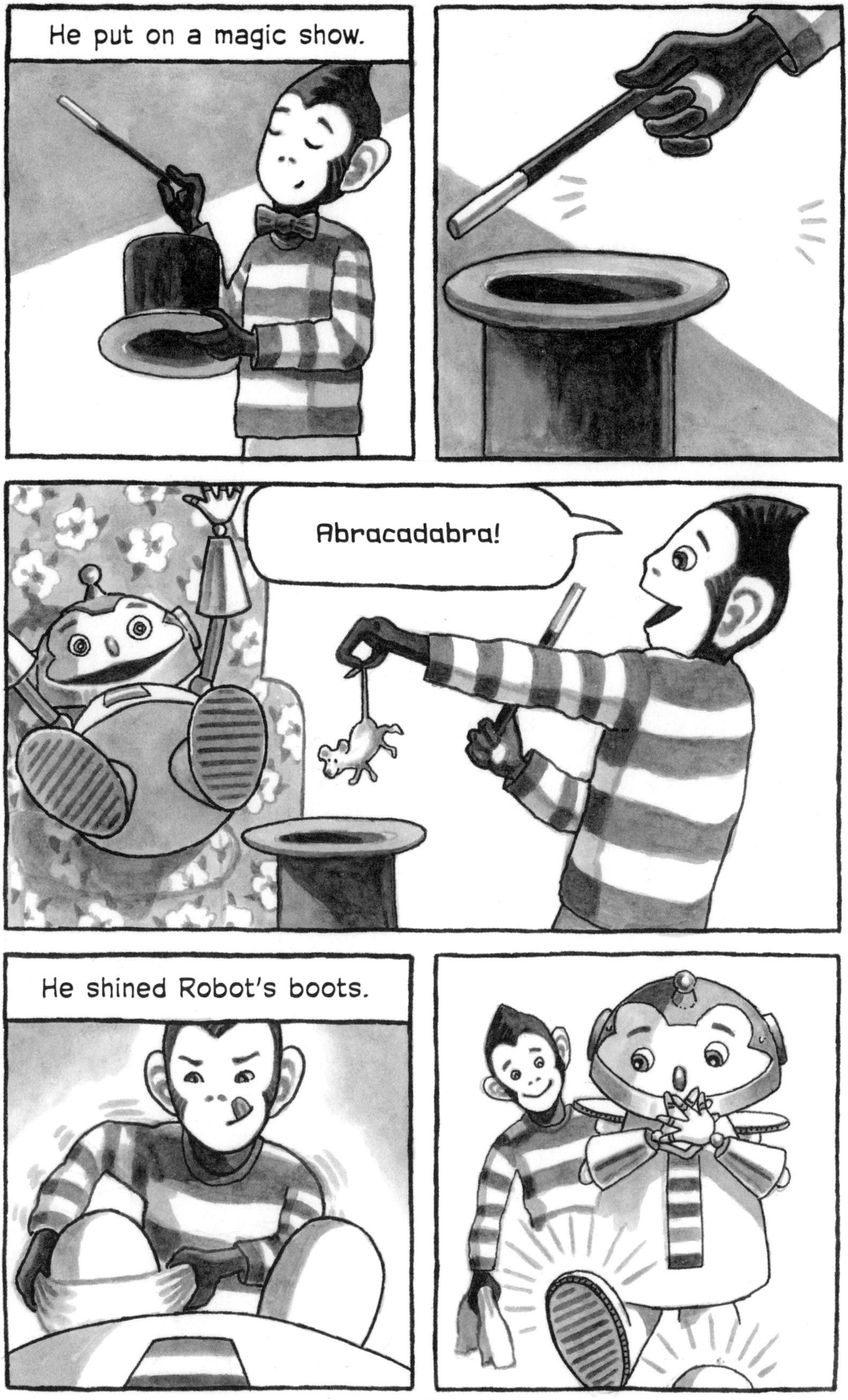
He put on a magic show.
Abracadabra!
He shined Robot's boots.

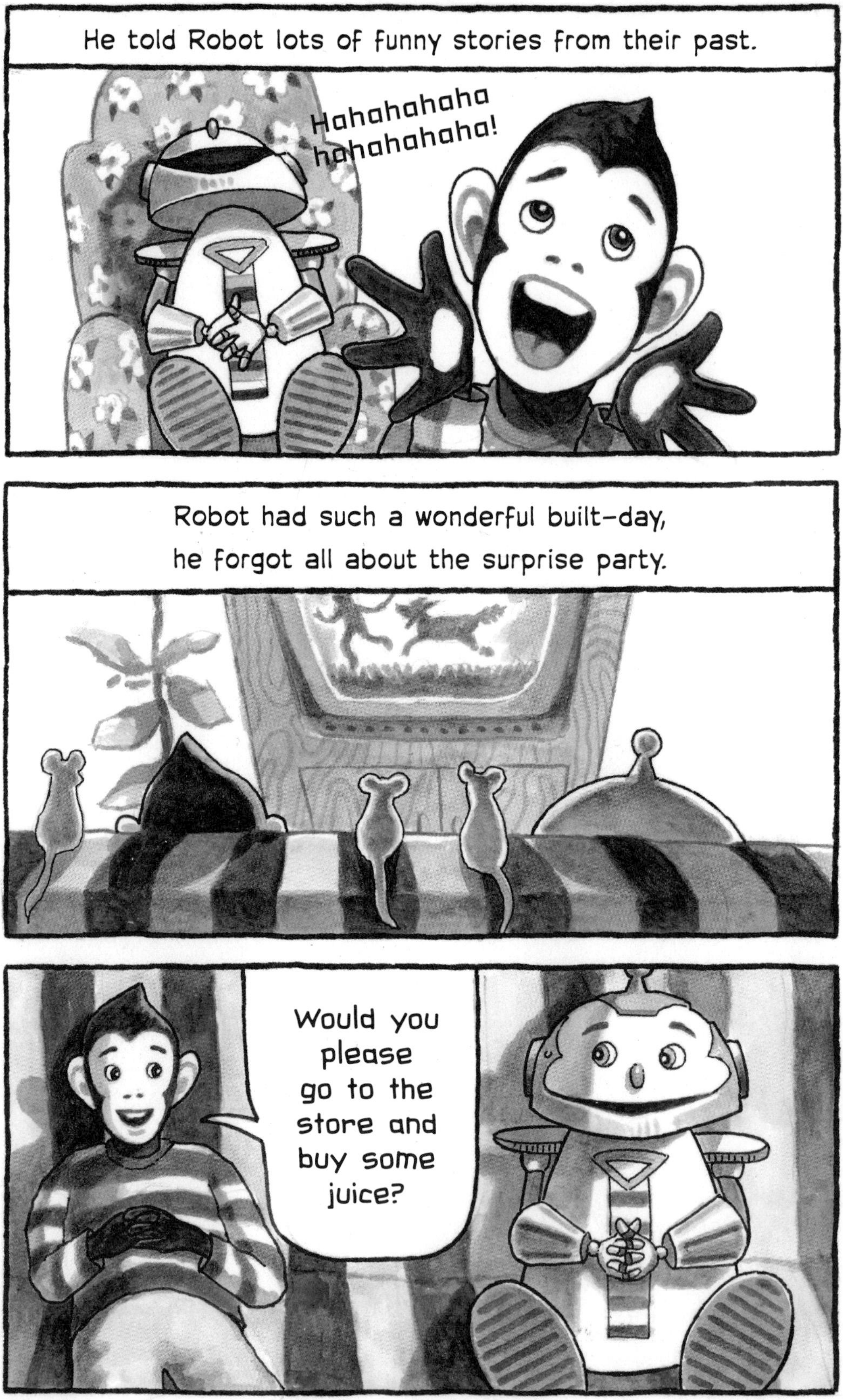
He told Robot lots of funny stories from their past.
Hahahahaha hahahahaha!
Robot had such a wonderful built-day, he forgot all about the surprise party.
Would you please go to the store and buy some juice?

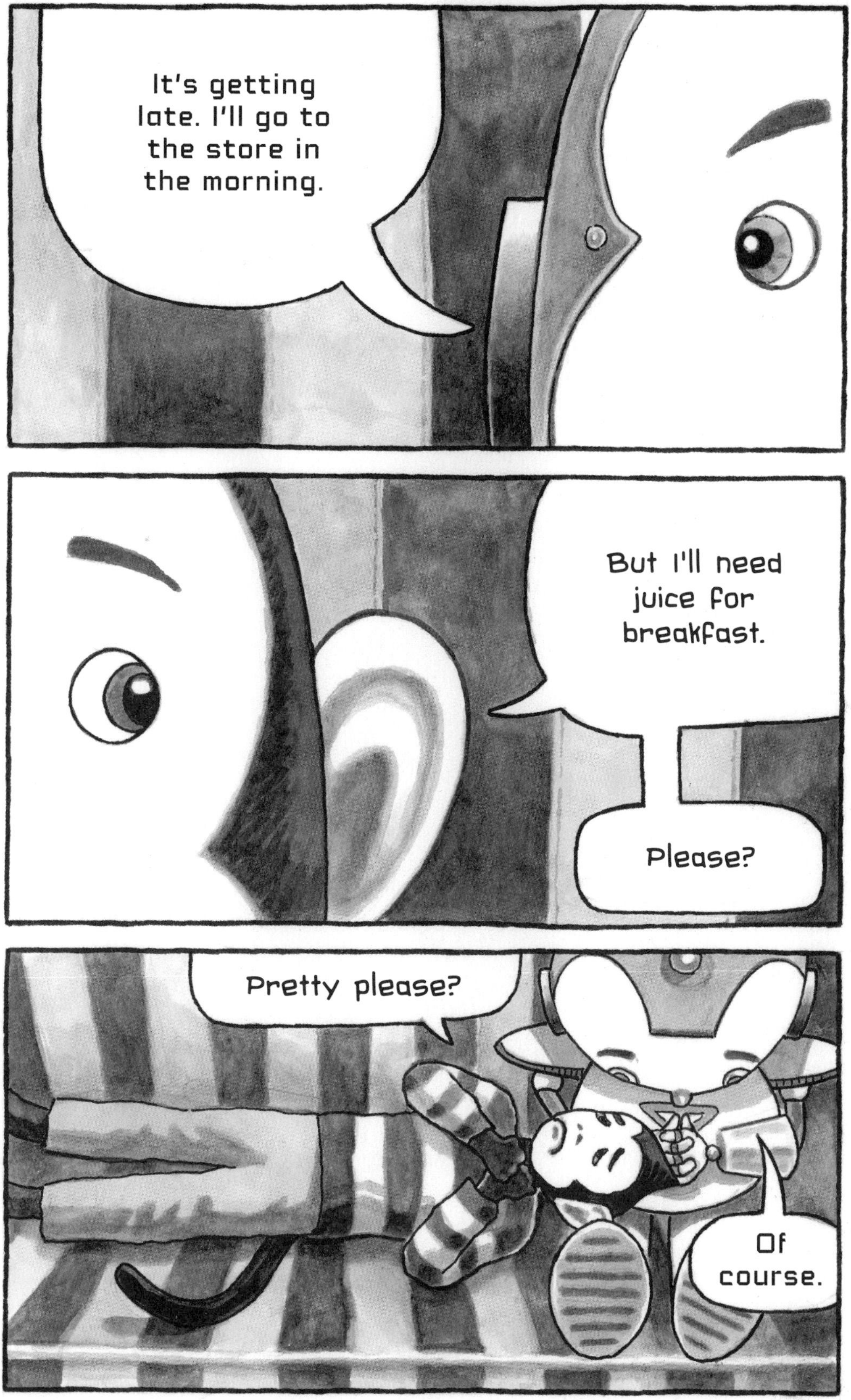
It's getting late. I'll go to the store in the morning.
But I'll need juice for breakfast.
Please?
Pretty please?
Of course.

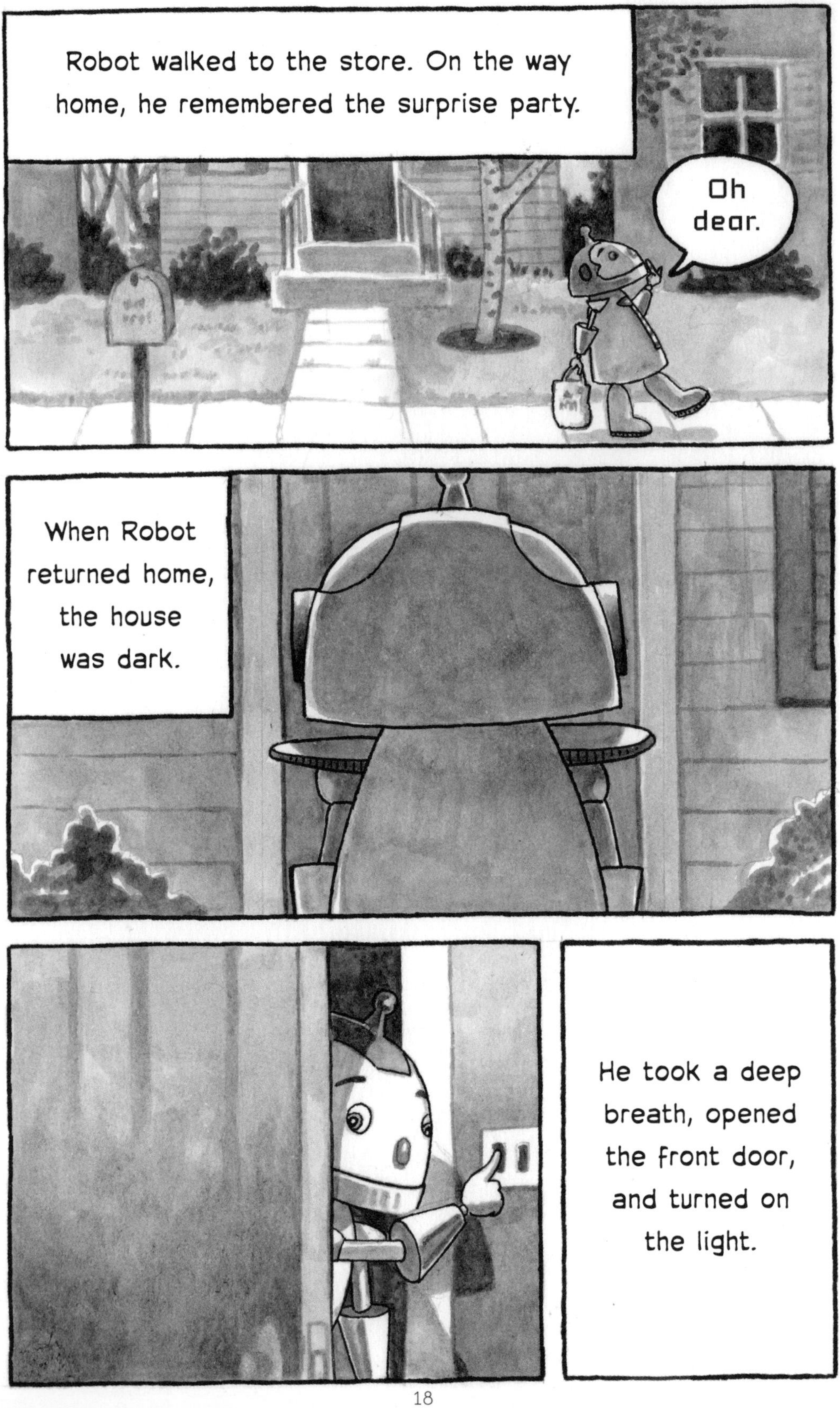
Robot walked to the store. On the way home, he remembered the surprise party.
Oh dear.
When Robot returned home, the house was dark.
He took a deep breath, opened the front door, and turned on the light.

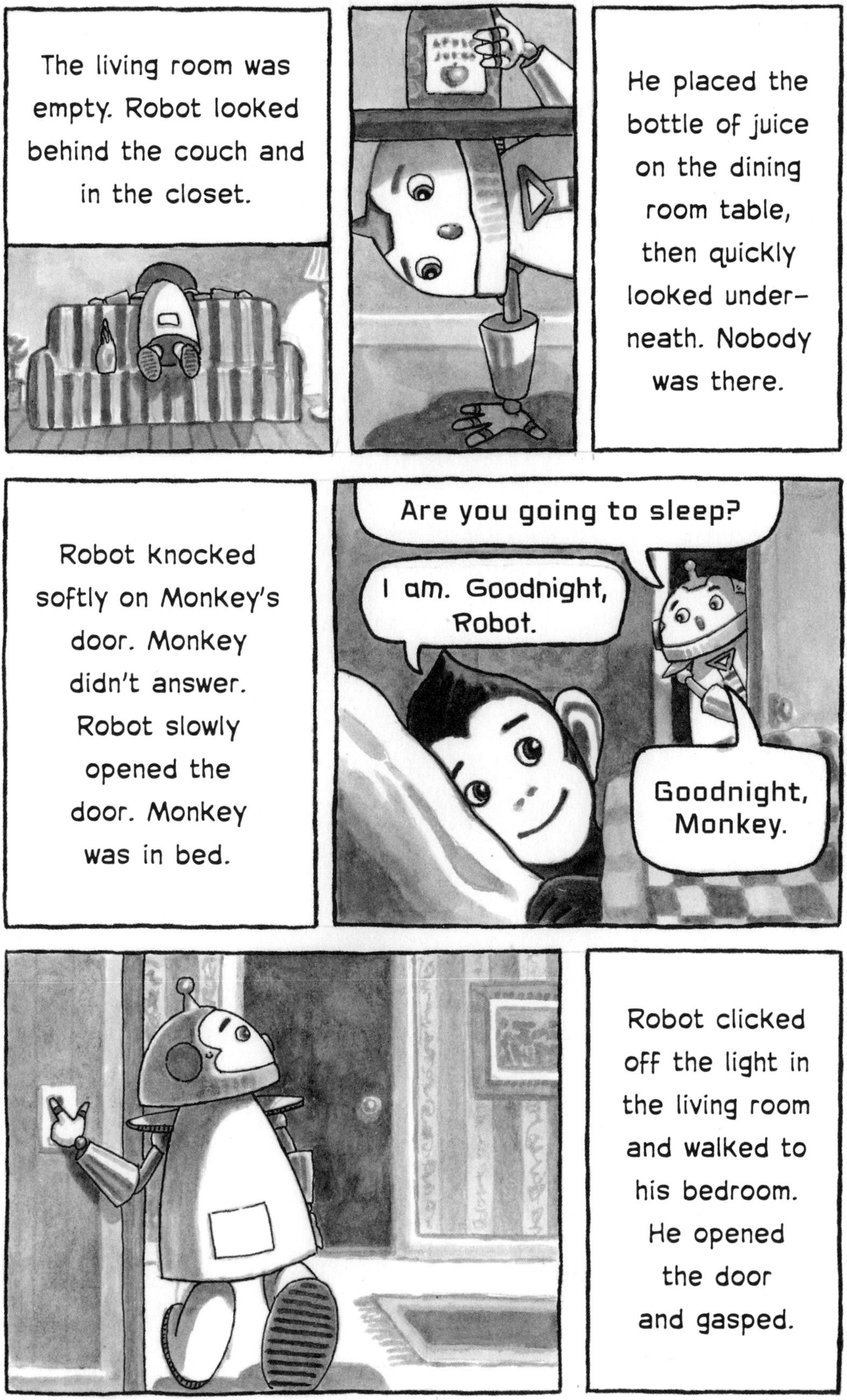
The living room was empty. Robot looked behind the couch and in the closet.
He placed the bottle of juice on the dining room table, then quickly looked underneath. Nobody was there.
Robot knocked softly on Monkey's door. Monkey didn't answer. Robot slowly opened the door. Monkey was in bed.
Are you going to sleep?
I am. Goodnight, Robot.
Goodnight, Monkey.
Robot clicked off the light in the living room and walked to his bedroom. He opened the door and gasped.

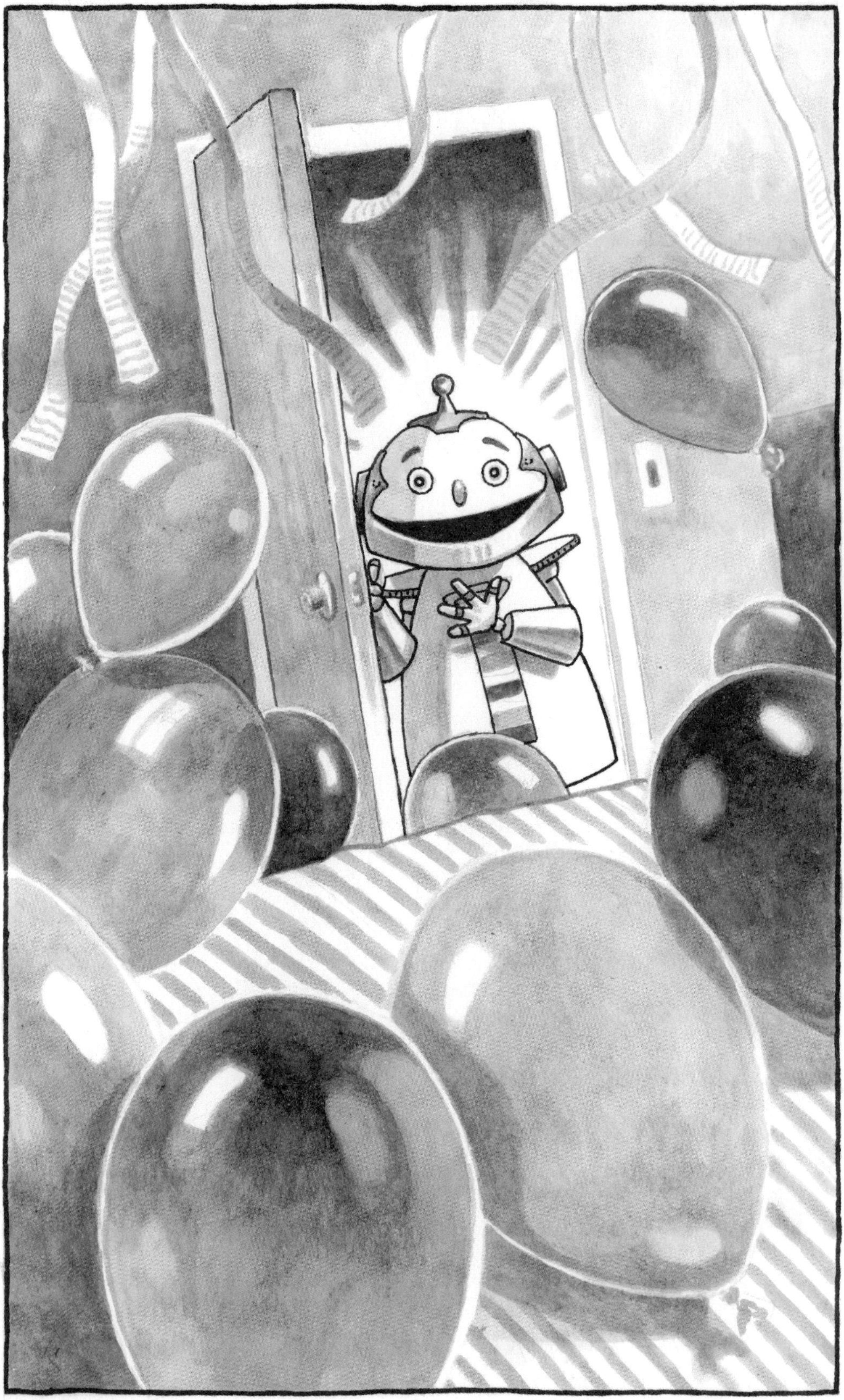

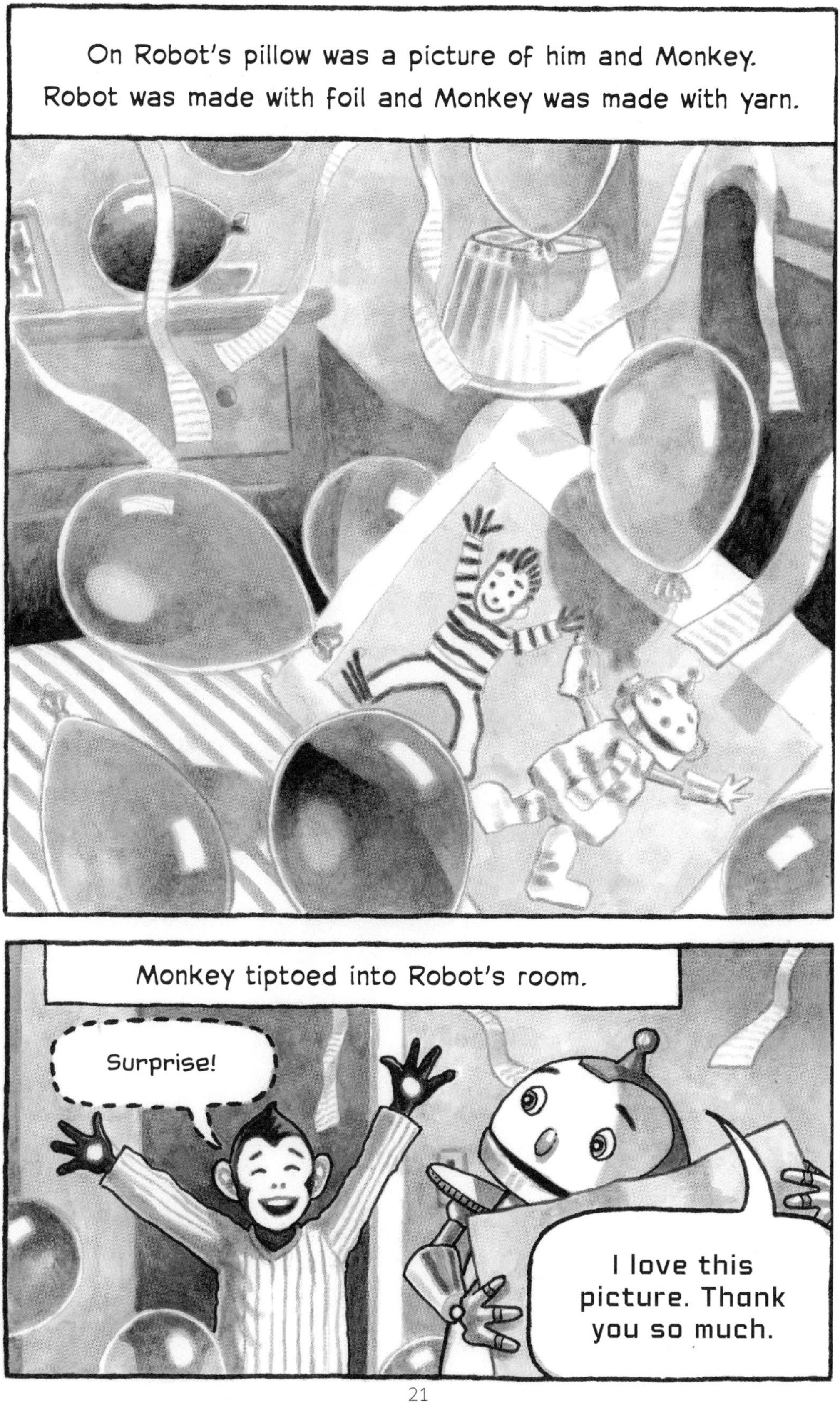
On Robot's pillow was a picture of him and Monkey.
Robot was made with foil and Monkey was made with yarn.
Monkey tiptoed into Robot's room.
Surprise!
I love this picture. Thank you so much.

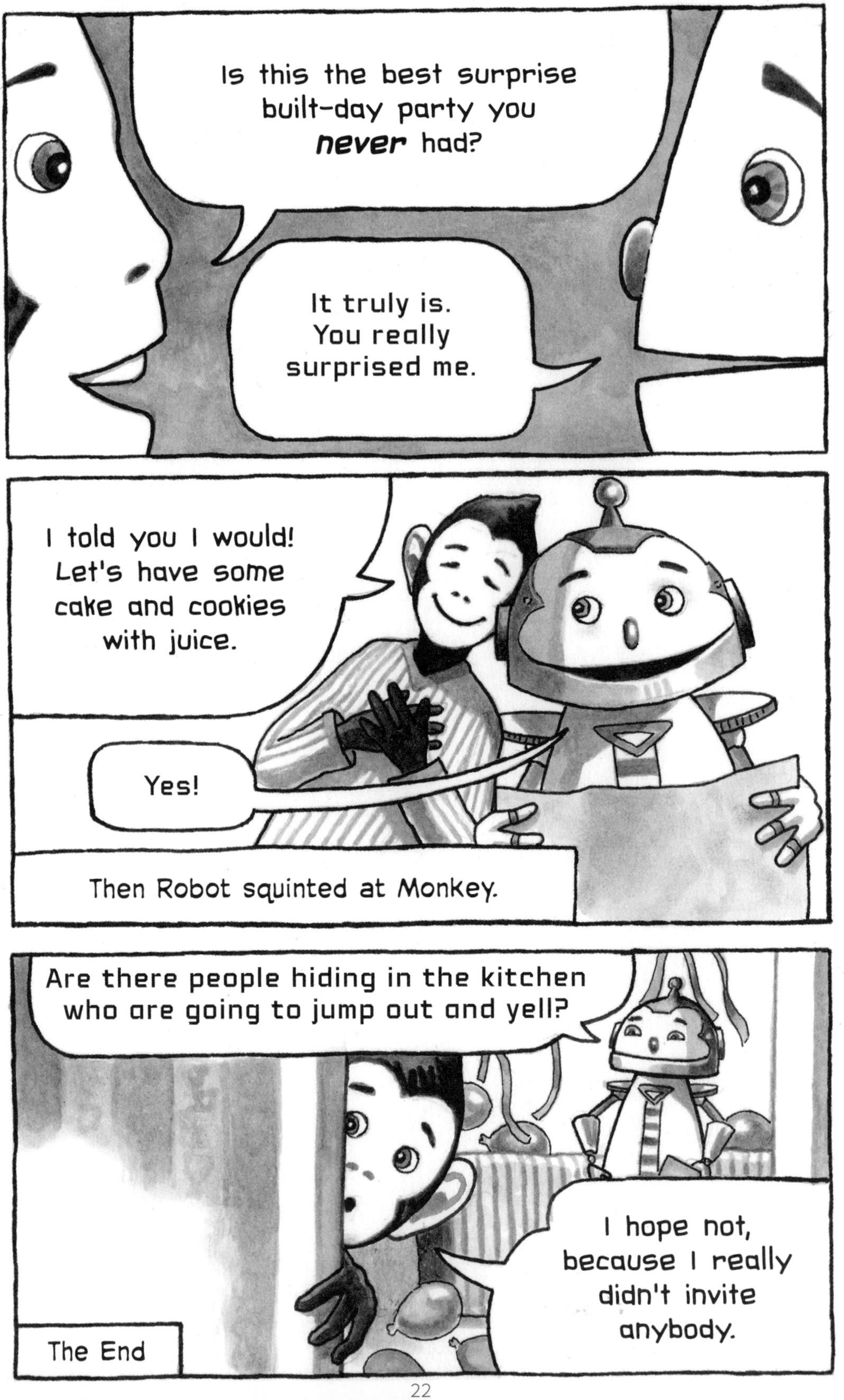
Is this the best surprise built-day party you ***never*** had?
It truly is. You really surprised me.
I told you I would! Let's have some cake and cookies with juice.
Yes!
Then Robot squinted at Monkey.
Are there people hiding in the kitchen who are going to jump out and yell?
I hope not, because I really didn't invite anybody.
The End

Cookies & Mice

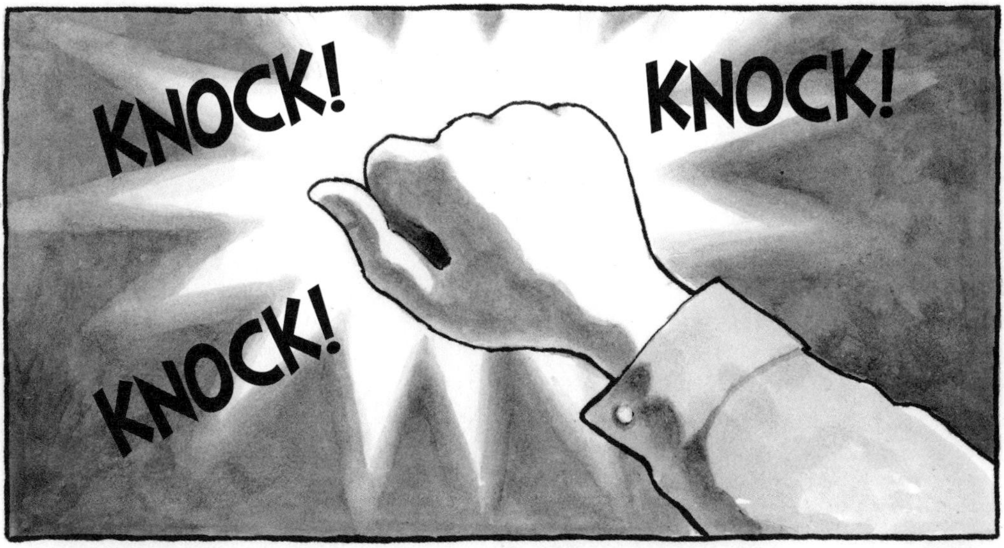
KNOCK!
KNOCK!
KNOCK!

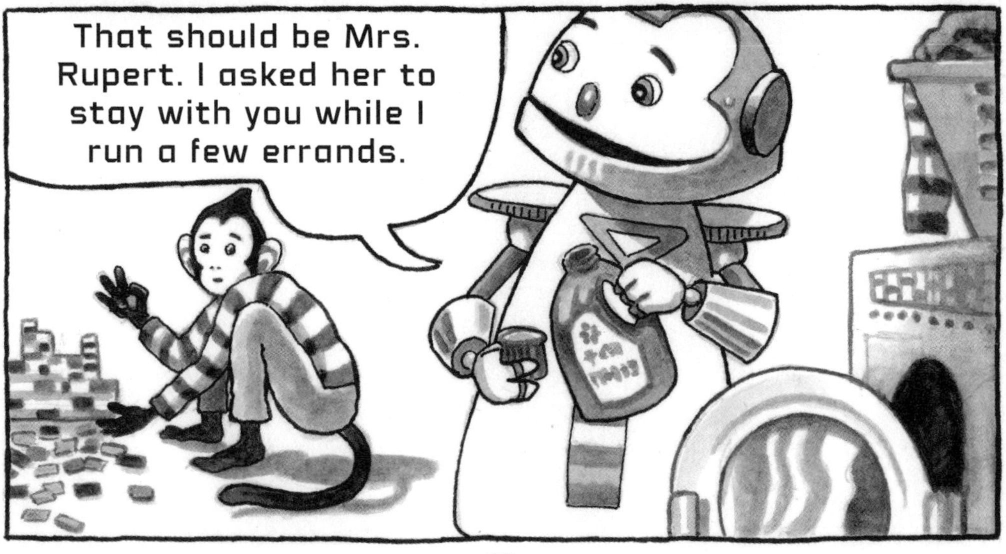
That should be Mrs. Rupert. I asked her to stay with you while I run a few errands.

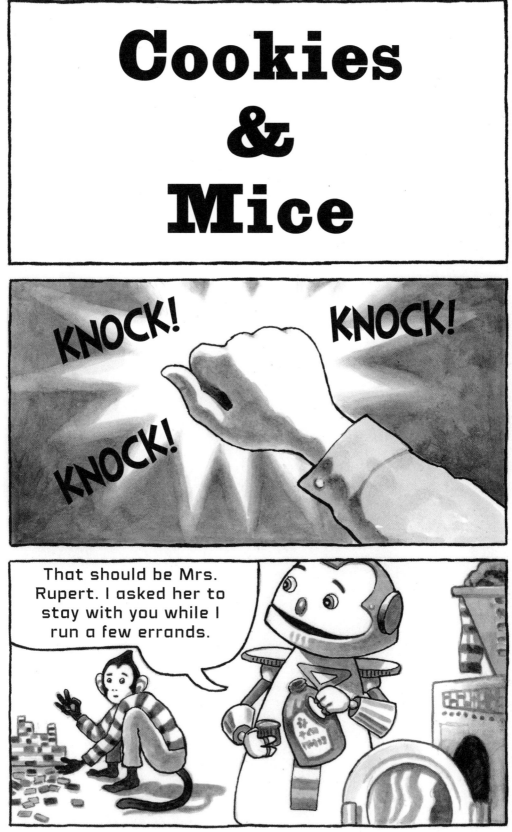

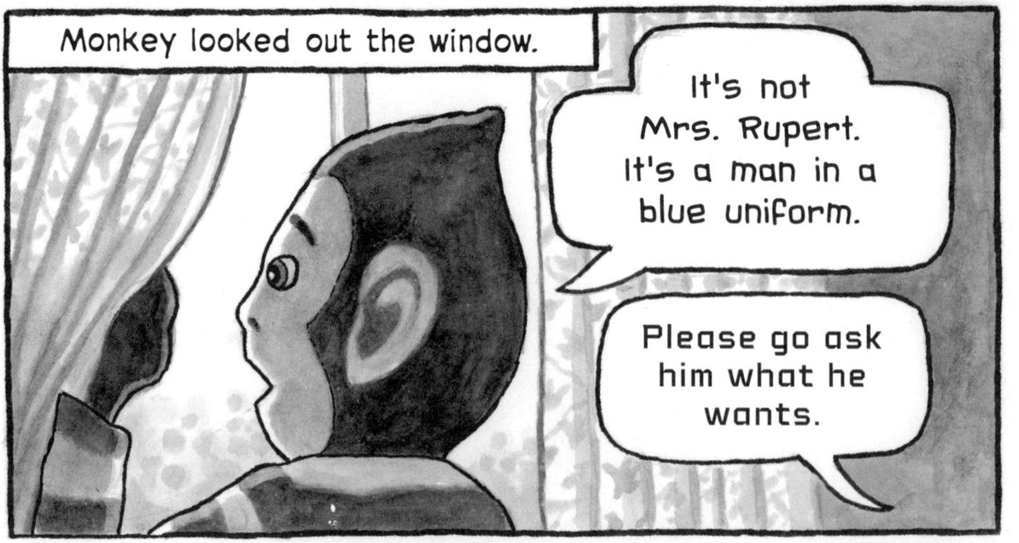
Monkey looked out the window.
It's not Mrs. Rupert. It's a man in a blue uniform.
Please go ask him what he wants.

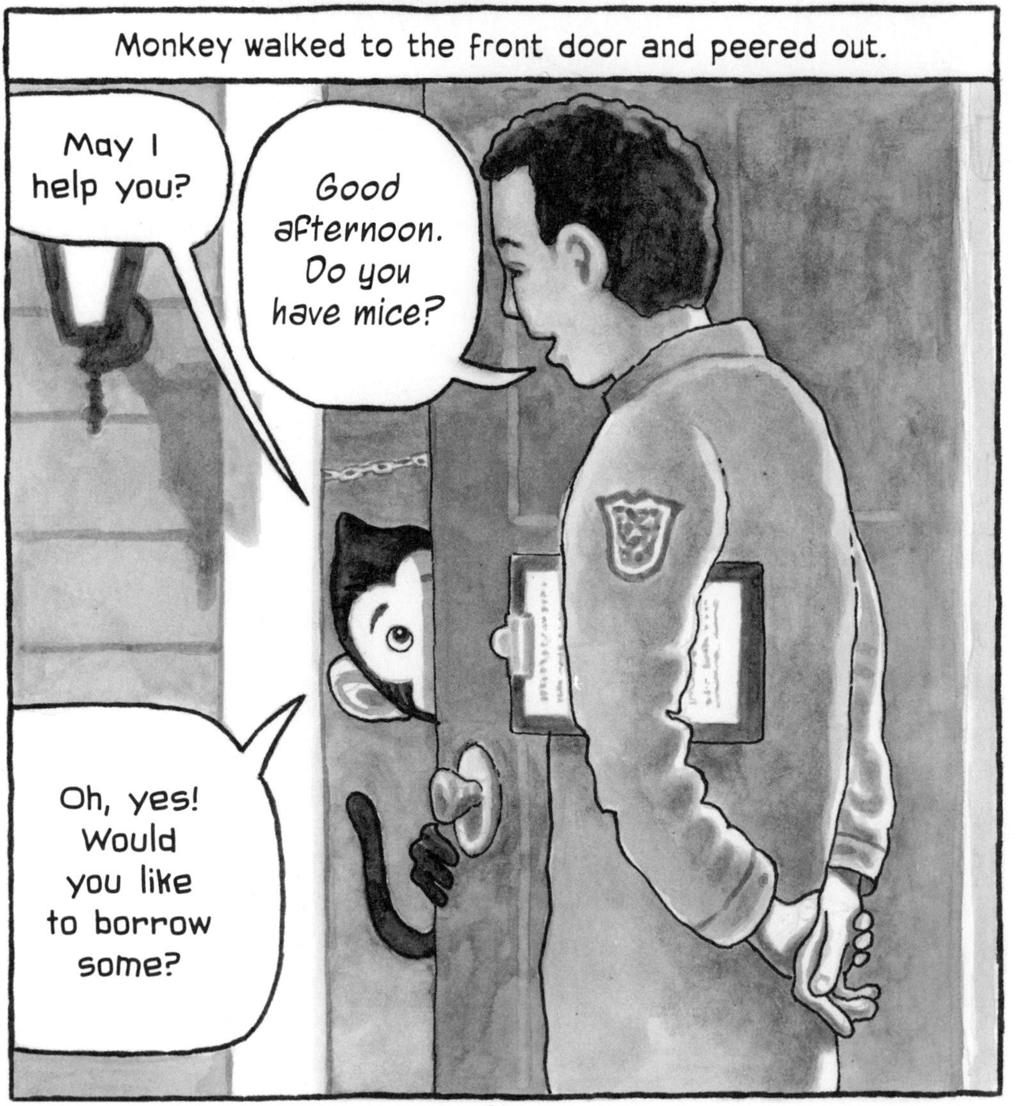
Monkey walked to the front door and peered out.
May I help you?
Good afternoon. Do you have mice?
Oh, yes! Would you like to borrow some?

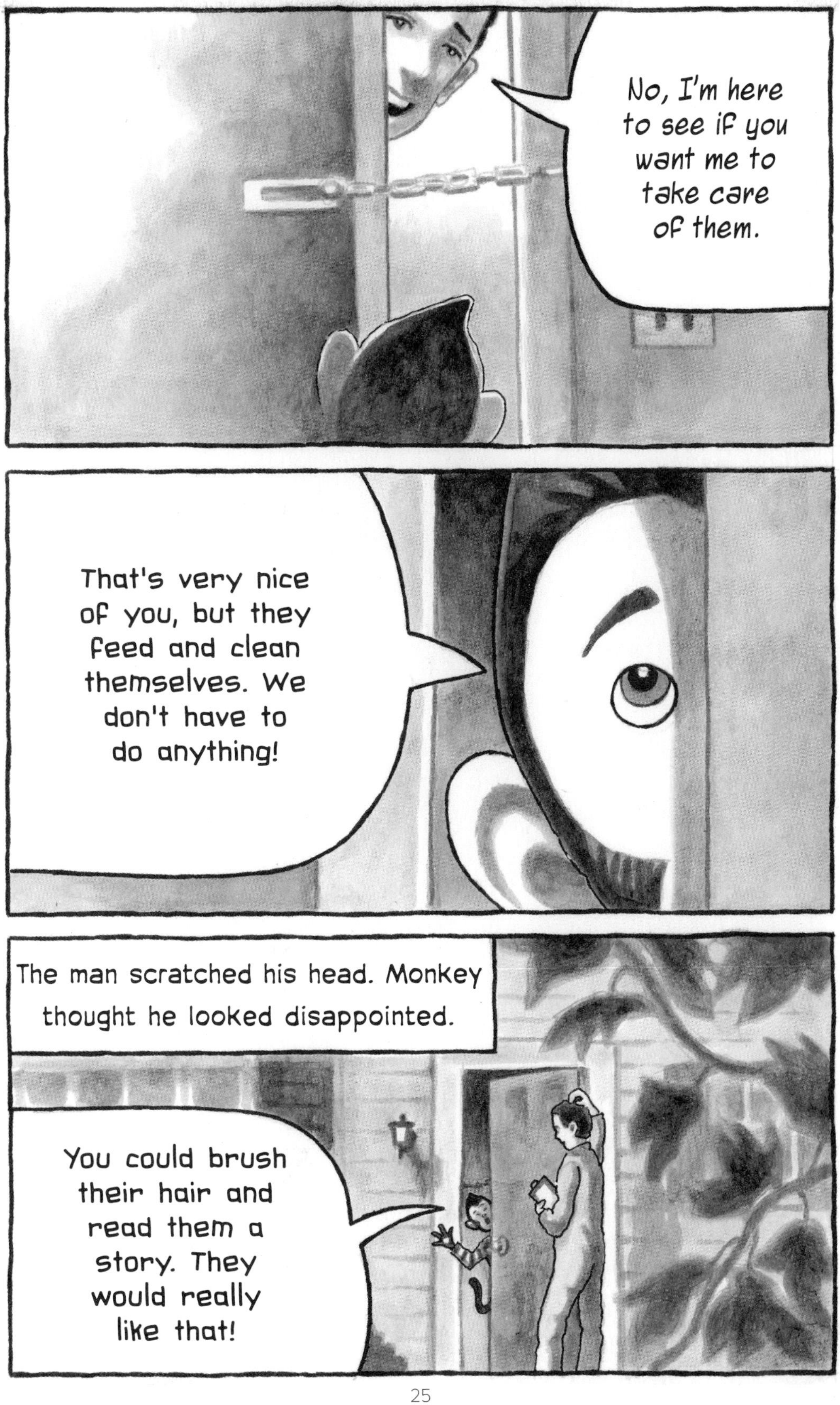
No, I'm here to see if you want me to take care of them.
That's very nice of you, but they feed and clean themselves. We don't have to do anything!
The man scratched his head. Monkey thought he looked disappointed.
You could brush their hair and read them a story. They would really like that!

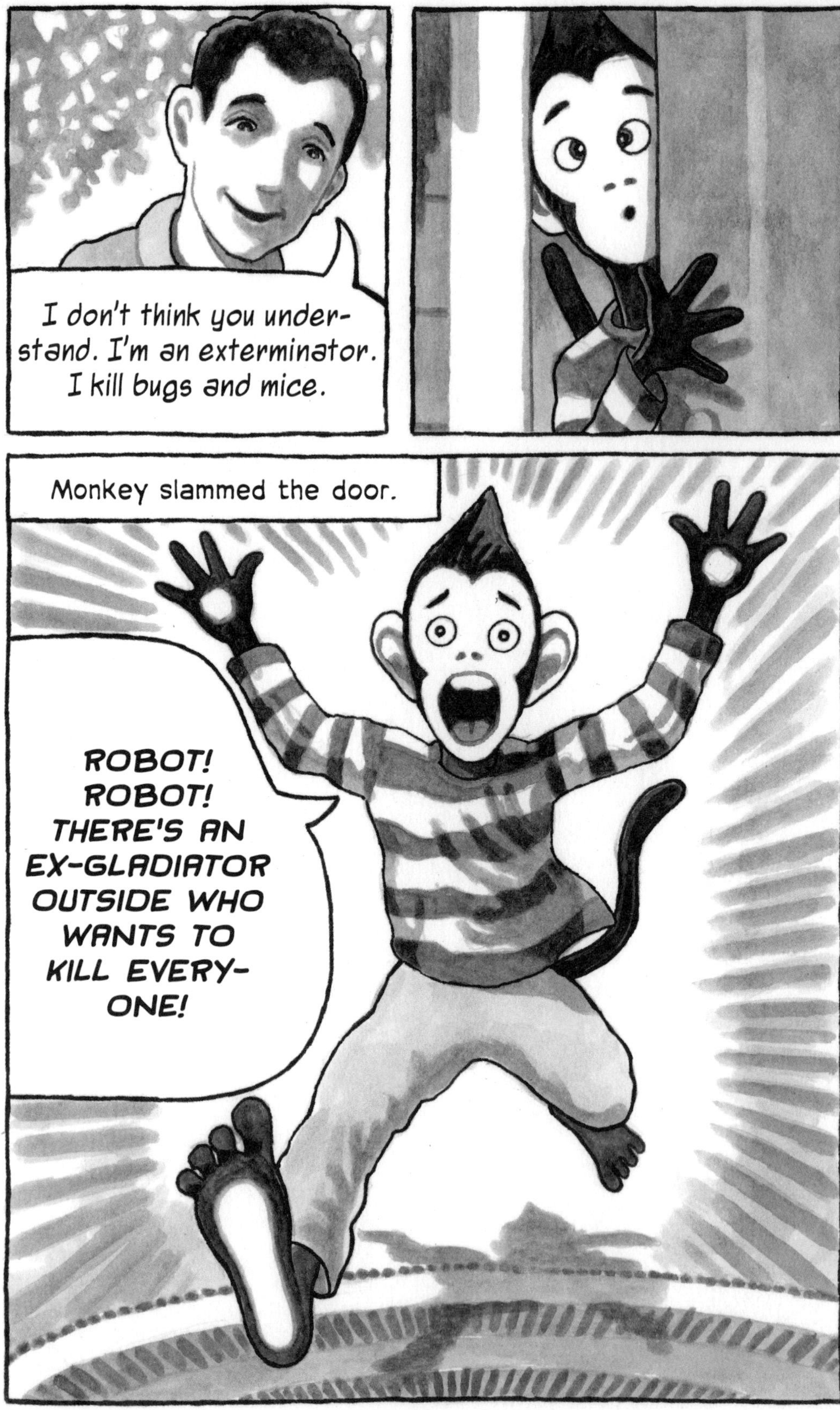
I don't think you under-stand. I'm an exterminator. I kill bugs and mice.
Monkey slammed the door.
ROBOT! ROBOT! THERE'S AN EX-GLADIATOR OUTSIDE WHO WANTS TO KILL EVERY-ONE!

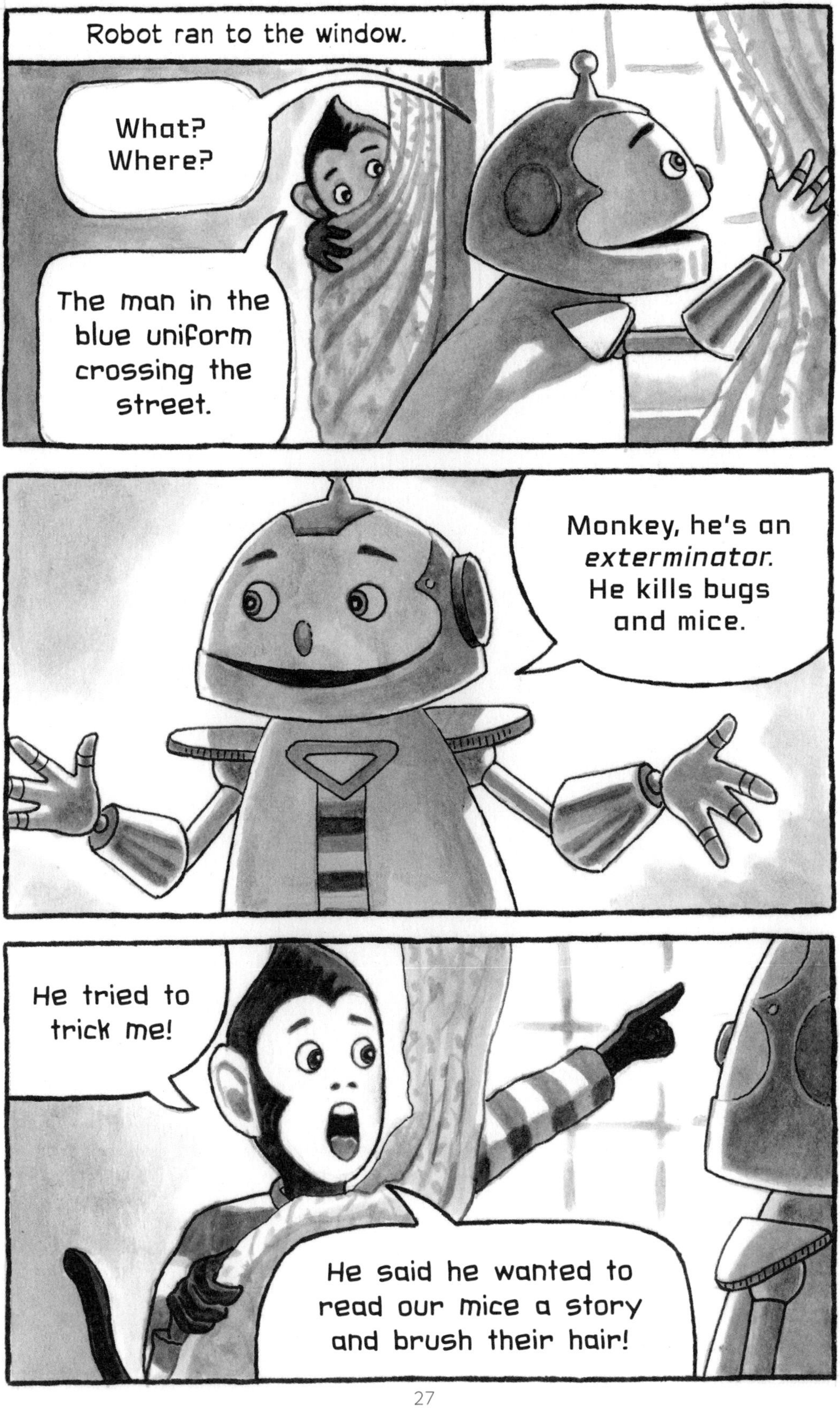
Robot ran to the window.
What? Where?
The man in the blue uniform crossing the street.
Monkey, he's an *exterminator*. He kills bugs and mice.
He tried to trick me!
He said he wanted to read our mice a story and brush their hair!

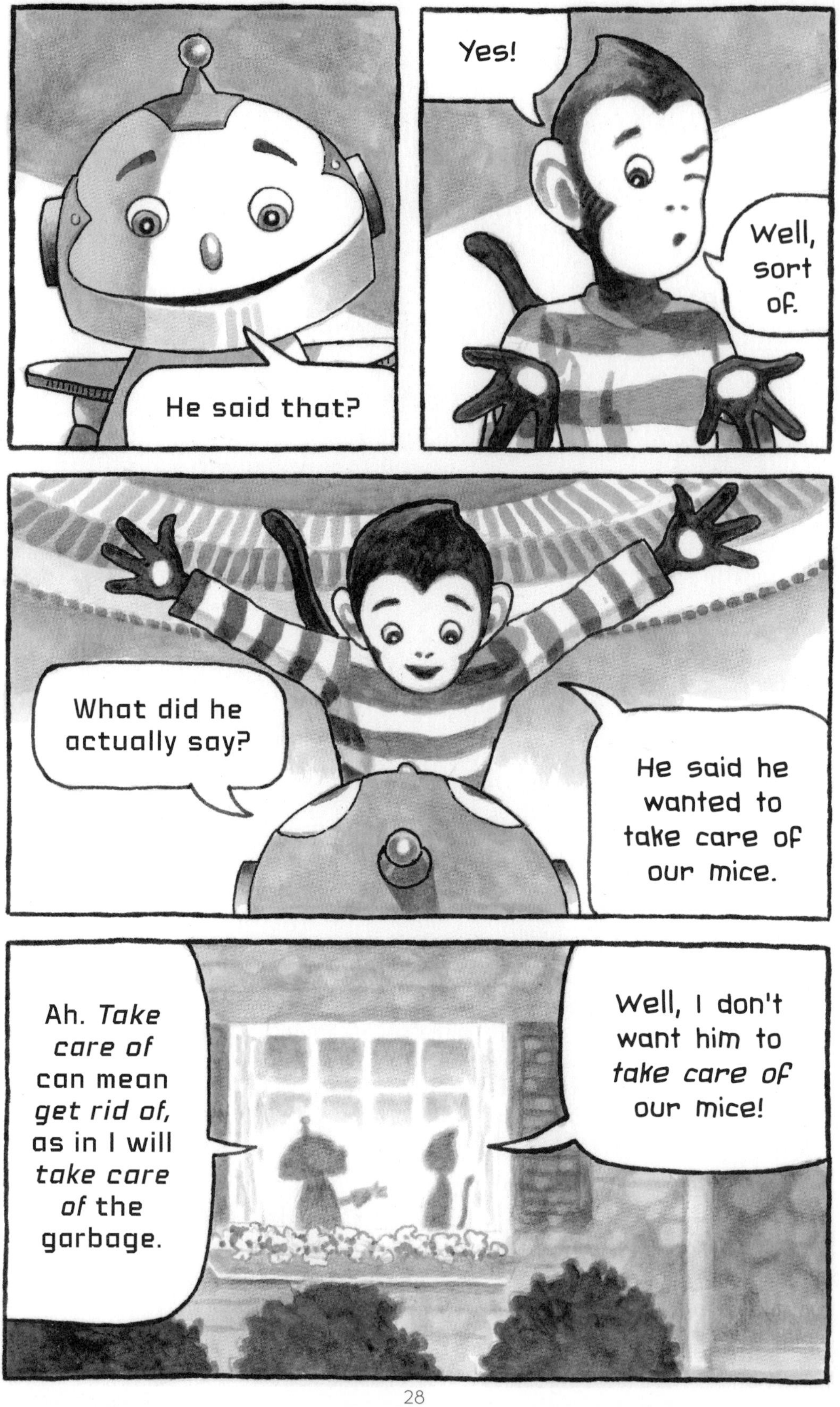
He said that?
Yes!
Well, sort of.
What did he actually say?
He said he wanted to take care of our mice.
Ah. *Take care of* can mean *get rid of,* as in I will *take care of* the garbage.
Well, I don't want him to *take care of* our mice!

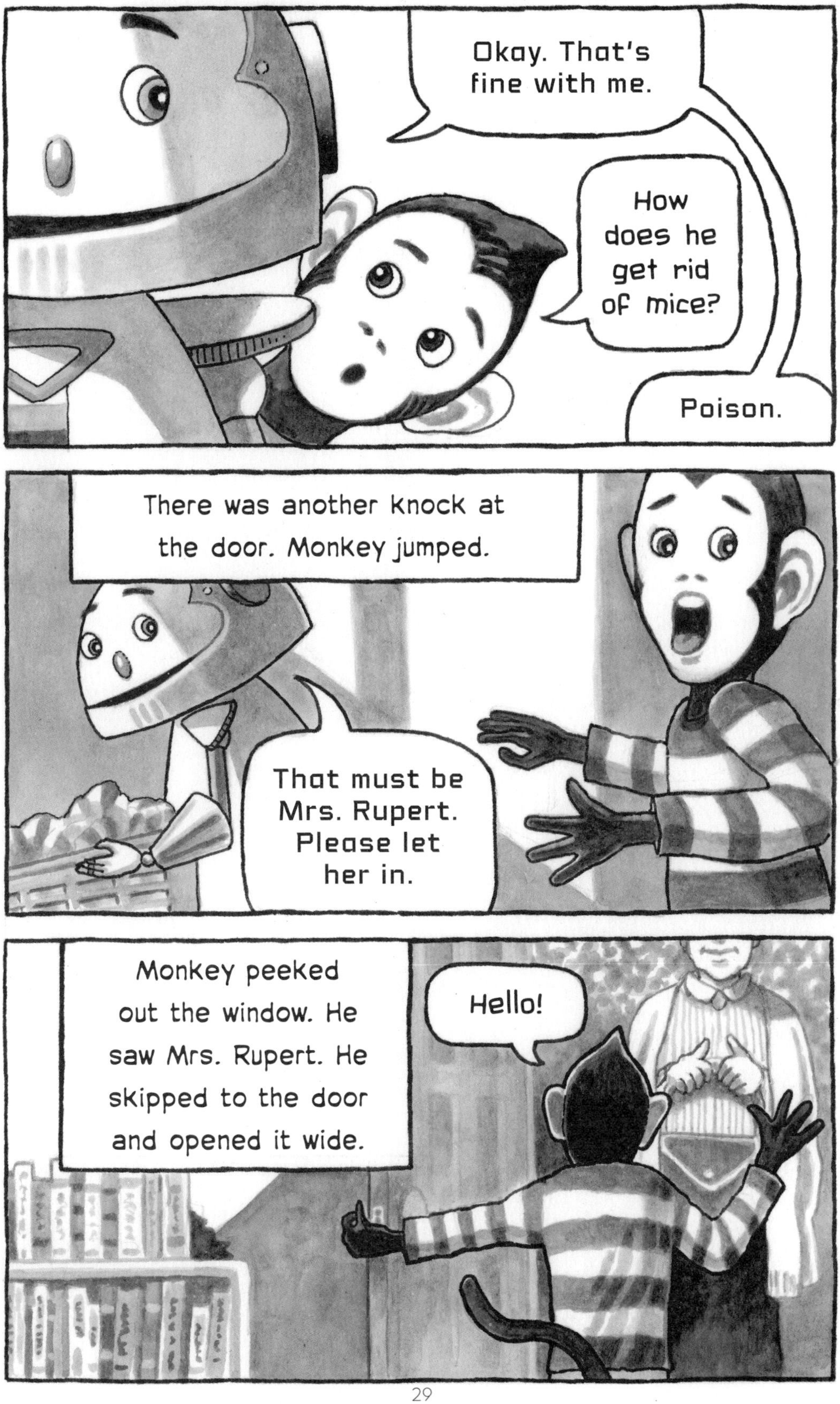
Okay. That's fine with me.
How does he get rid of mice?
Poison.
There was another knock at the door. Monkey jumped.
That must be Mrs. Rupert. Please let her in.
Monkey peeked out the window. He saw Mrs. Rupert. He skipped to the door and opened it wide.
Hello!

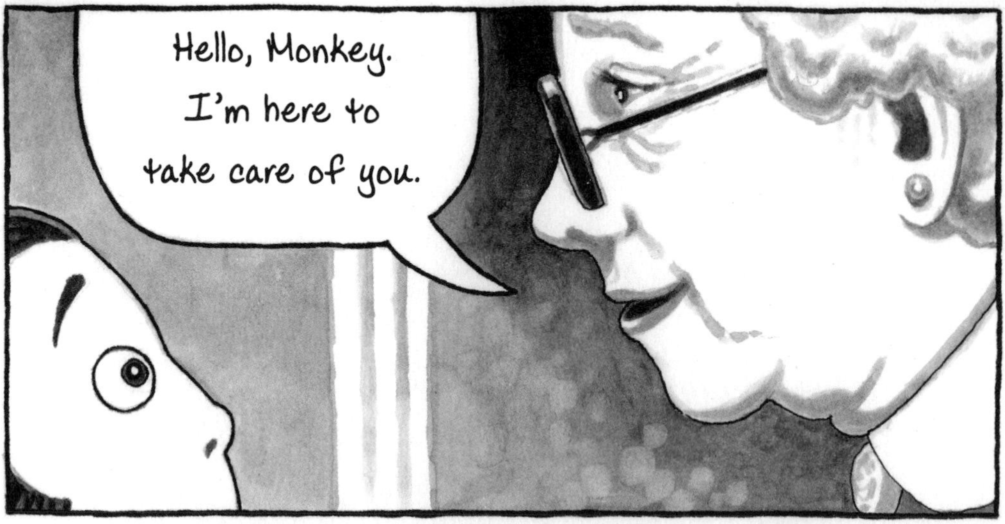
Hello, Monkey.
I'm here to
take care of you.

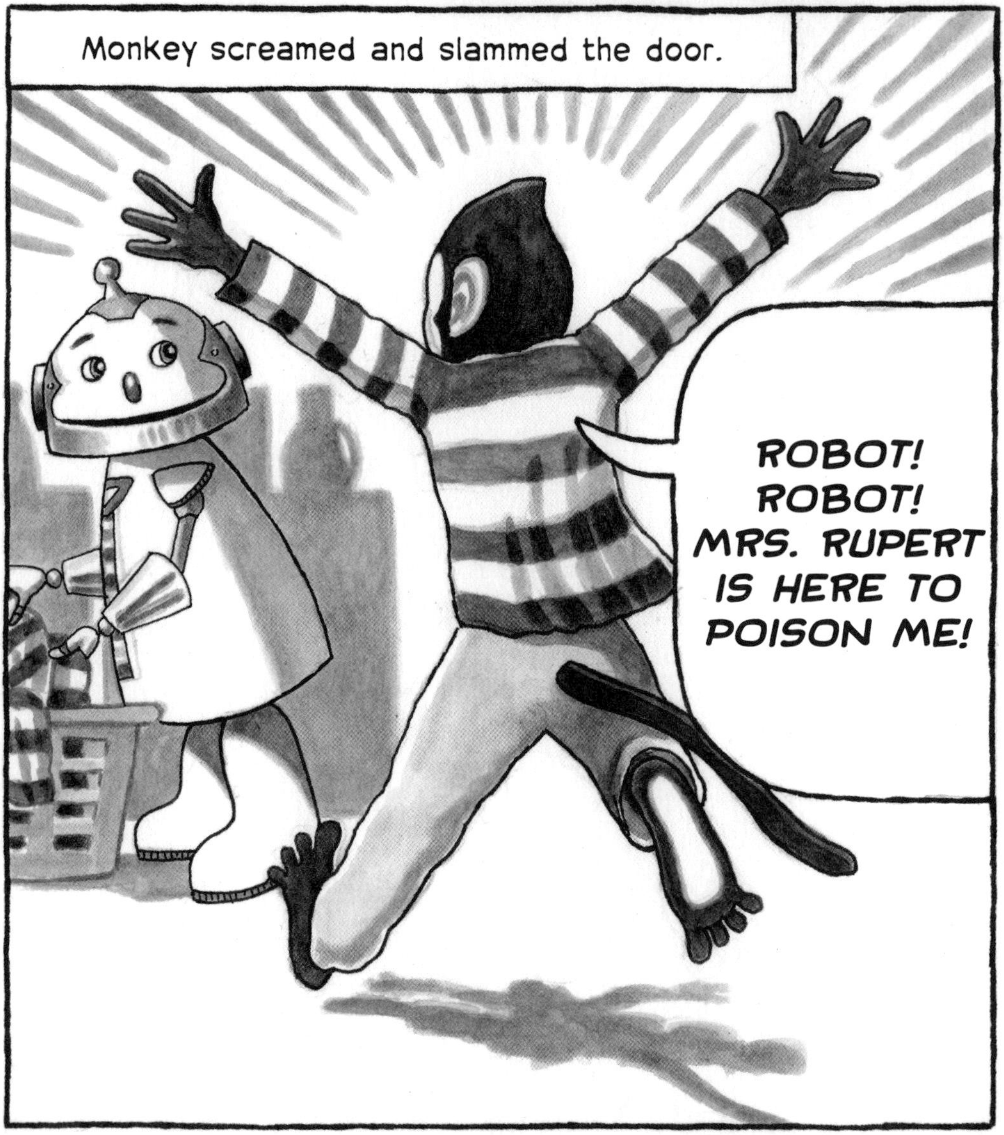
Monkey screamed and slammed the door.
ROBOT!
ROBOT!
MRS. RUPERT
IS HERE TO
POISON ME!

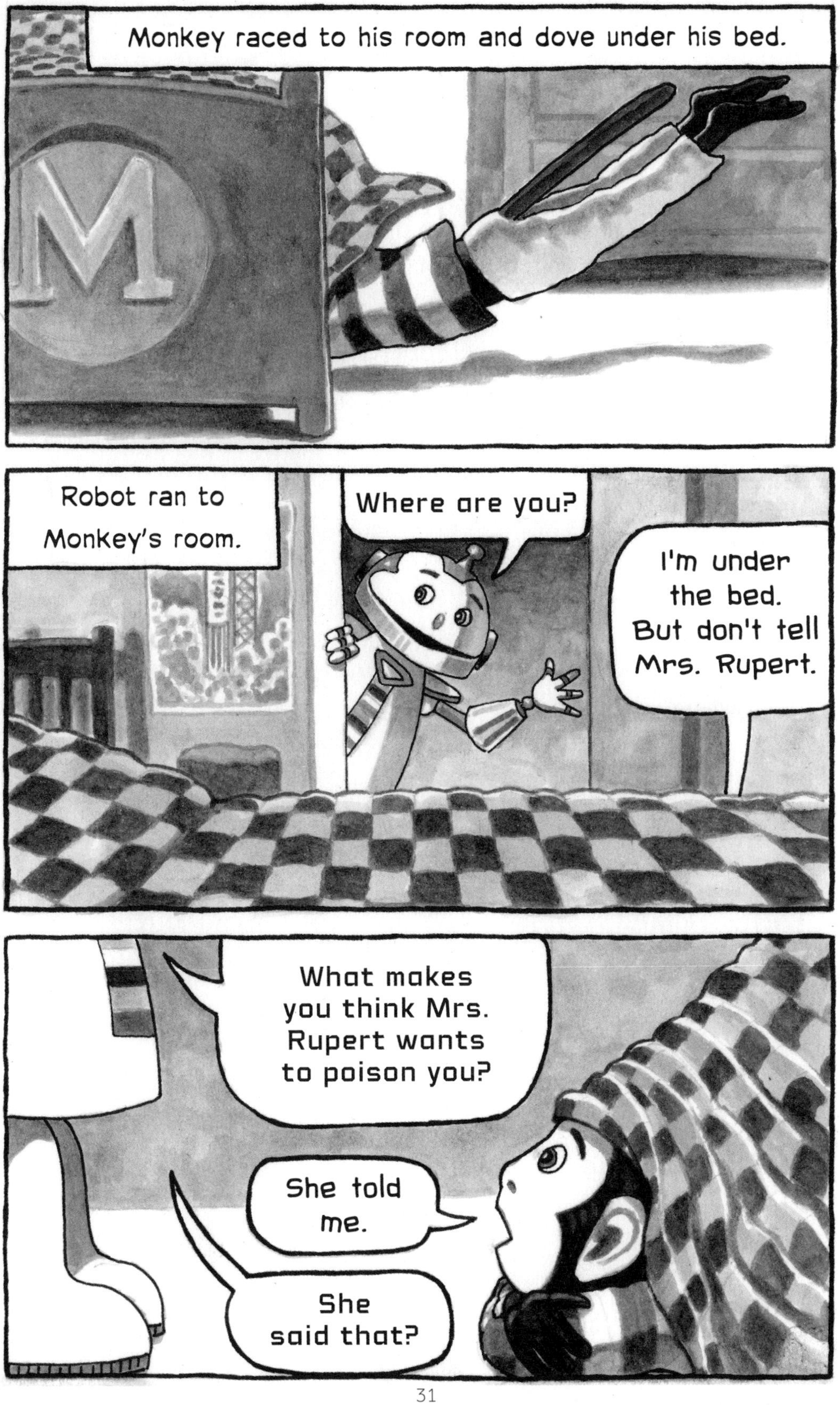
Monkey raced to his room and dove under his bed.
Robot ran to Monkey's room.
Where are you?
I'm under the bed. But don't tell Mrs. Rupert.
What makes you think Mrs. Rupert wants to poison you?
She told me.
She said that?

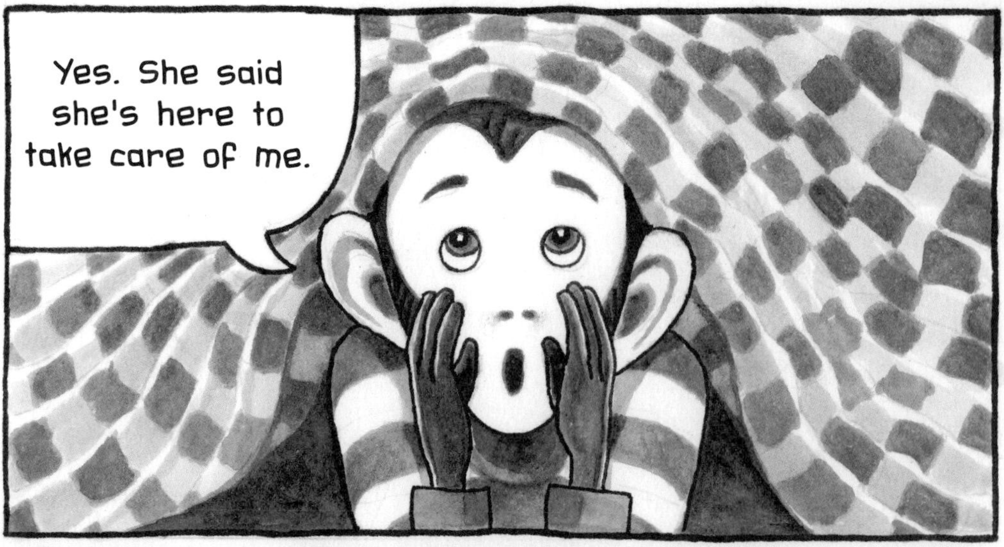
Yes. She said she's here to take care of me.

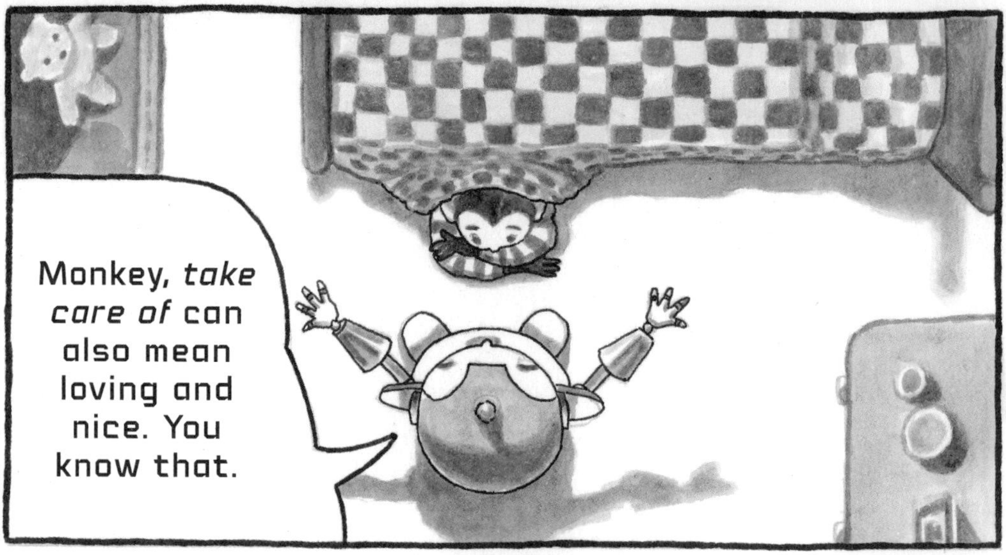
Monkey, *take care of* can also mean loving and nice. You know that.

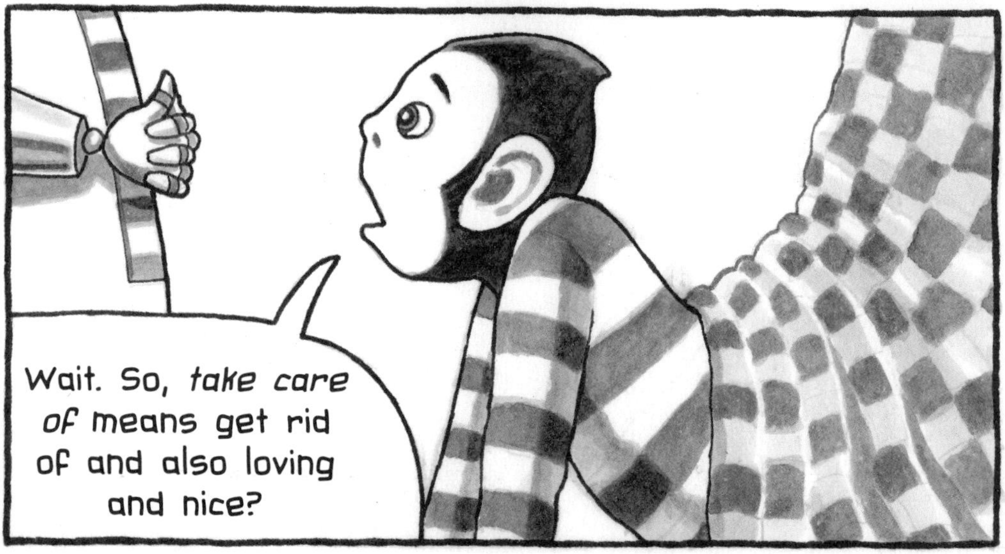
Wait. So, *take care of* means get rid of and also loving and nice?

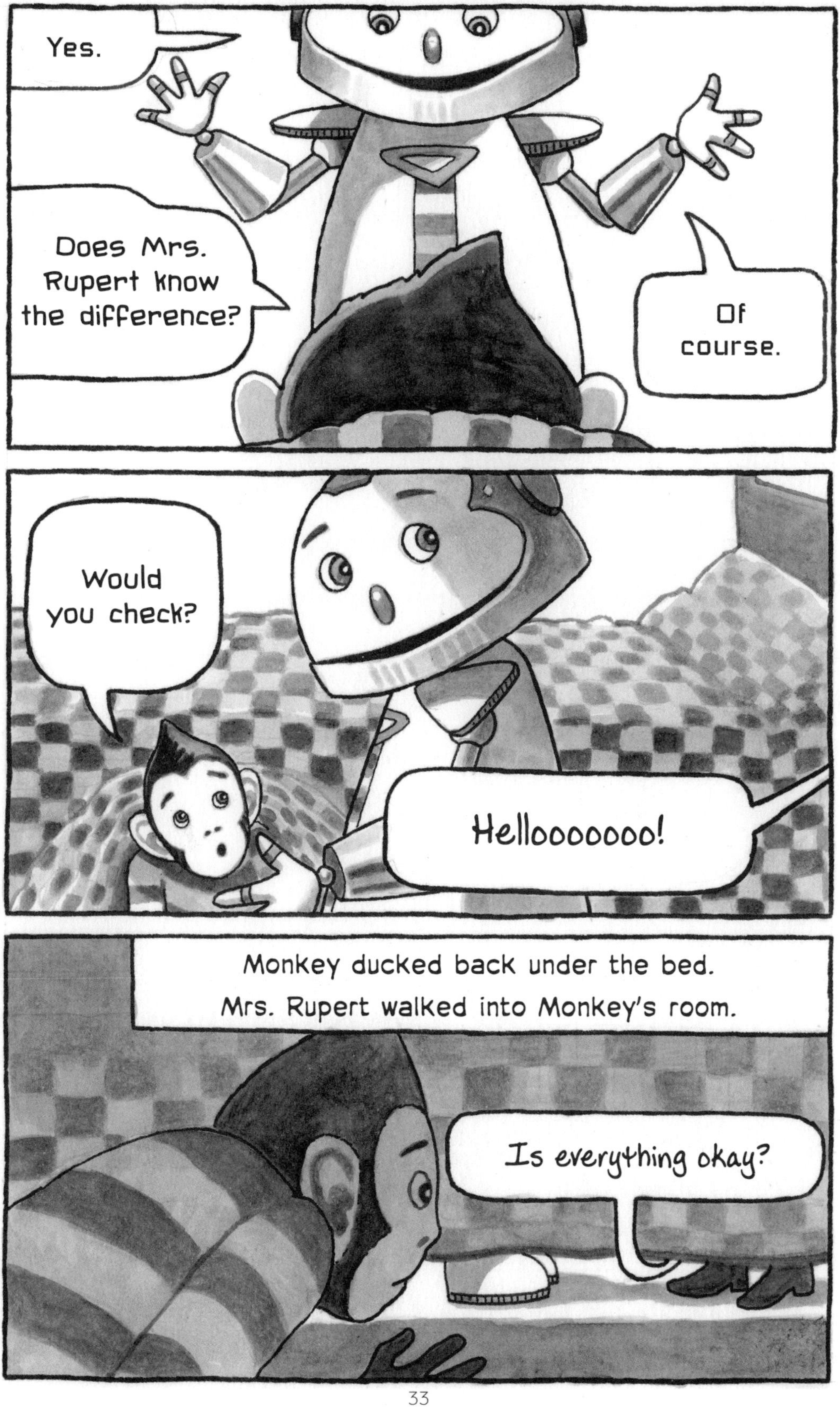
Yes.
Does Mrs. Rupert know the difference?
Of course.
Would you check?
Hellooooooo!
Monkey ducked back under the bed.
Mrs. Rupert walked into Monkey's room.
Is everything okay?

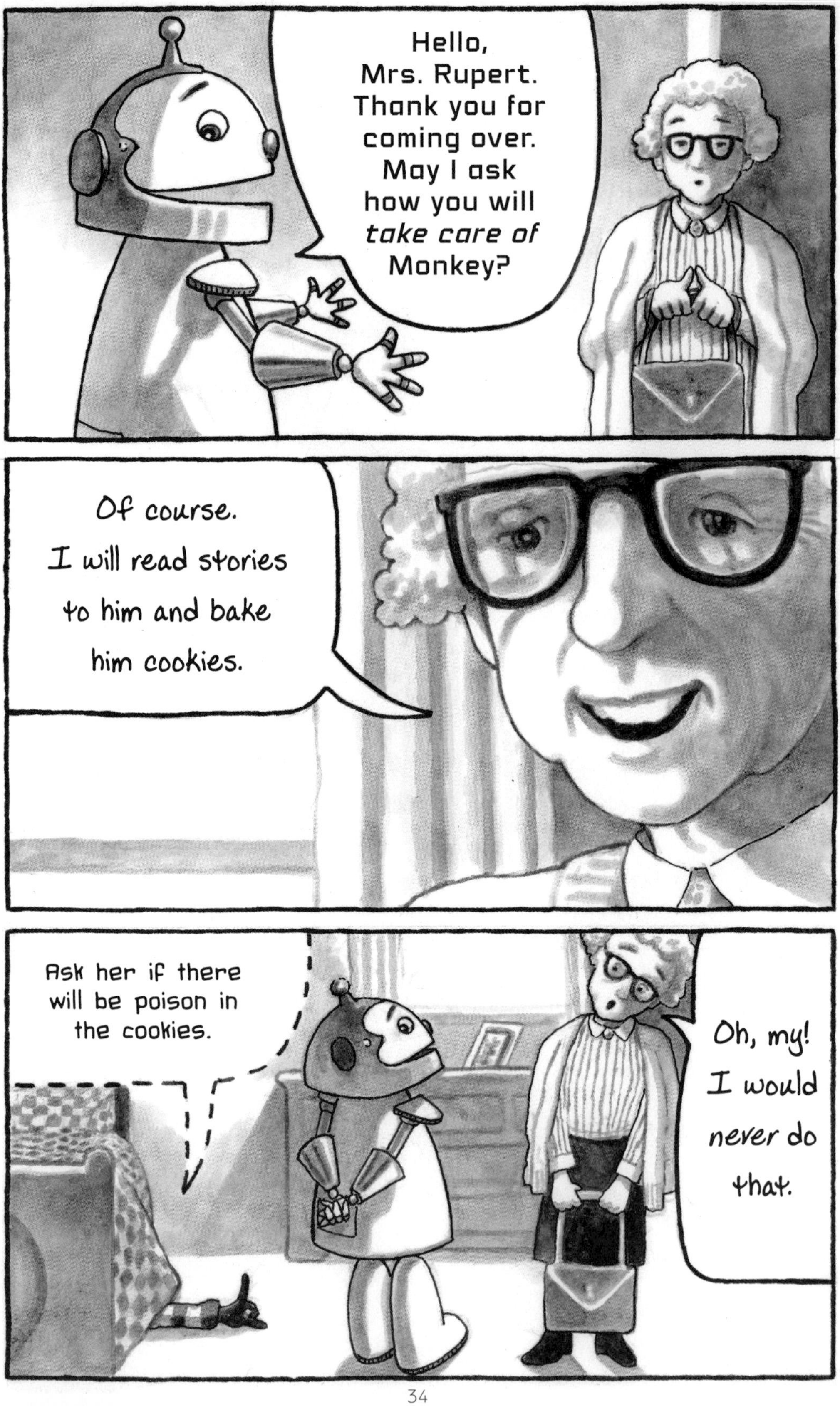
Hello, Mrs. Rupert. Thank you for coming over. May I ask how you will *take care of* Monkey?
Of course. I will read stories to him and bake him cookies.
Ask her if there will be poison in the cookies.
Oh, my! I would never do that.

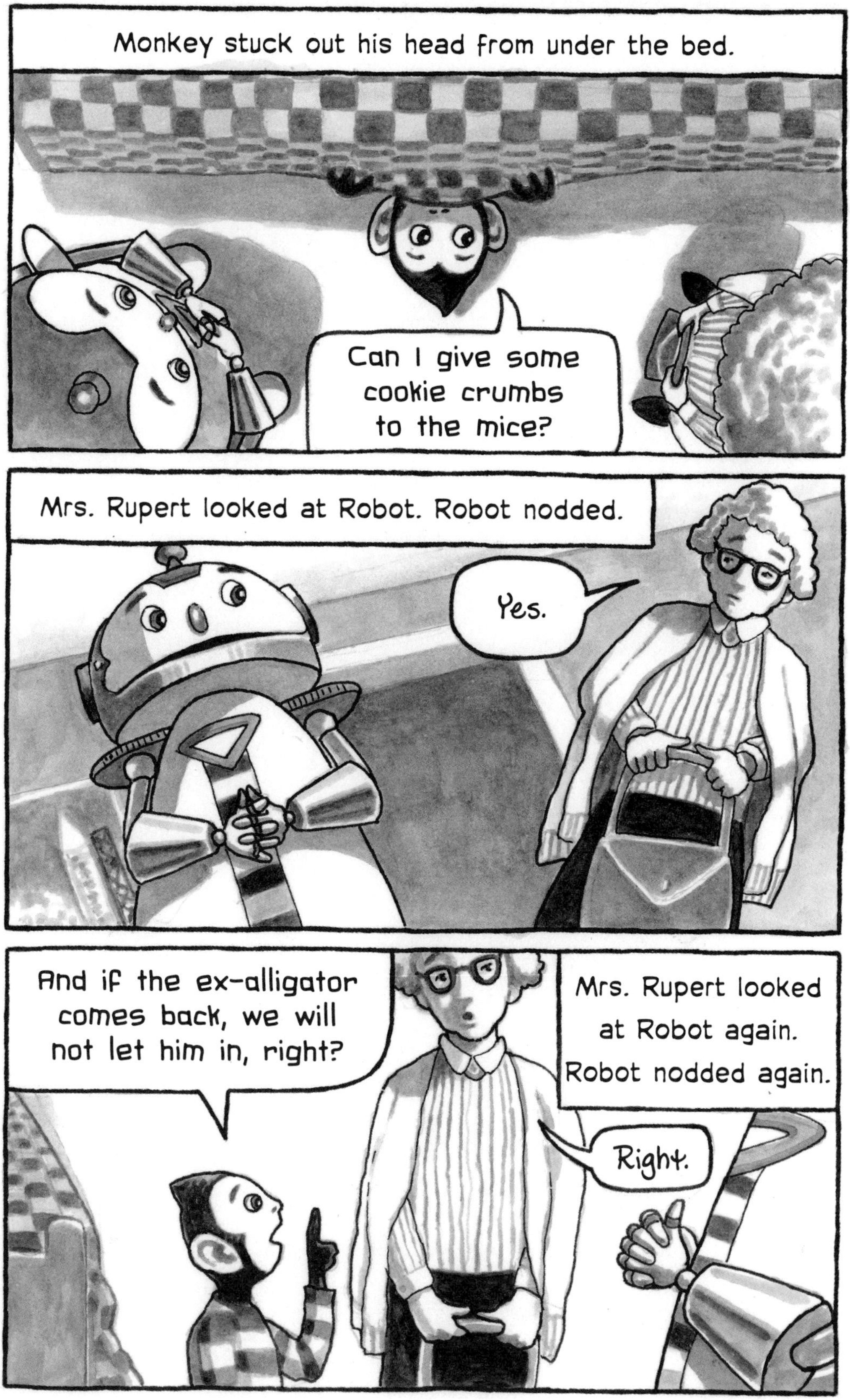
Monkey stuck out his head from under the bed.
Can I give some cookie crumbs to the mice?
Mrs. Rupert looked at Robot. Robot nodded.
Yes.
And if the ex-alligator comes back, we will not let him in, right?
Mrs. Rupert looked at Robot again. Robot nodded again.
Right.

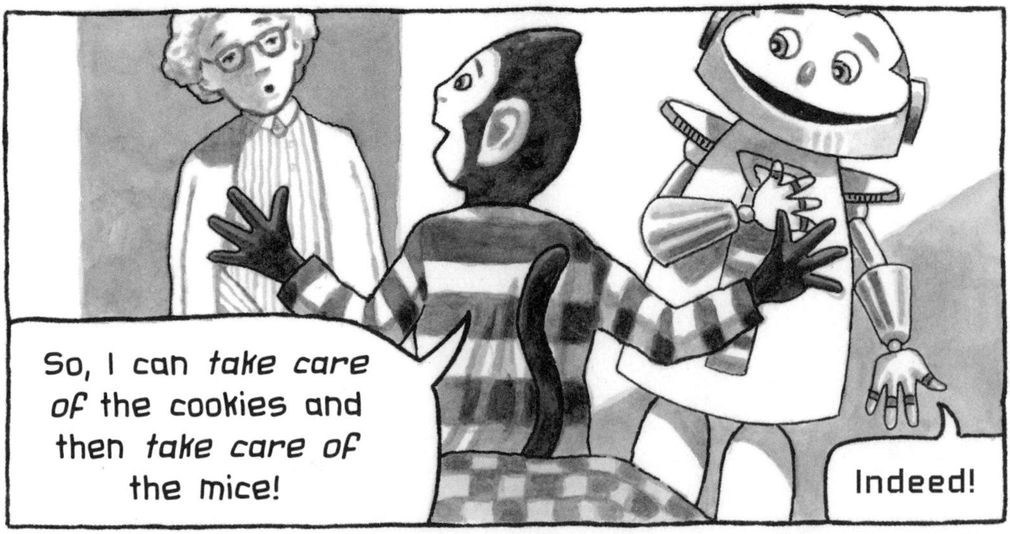
So, I can *take care of* the cookies and then *take care of* the mice!
Indeed!

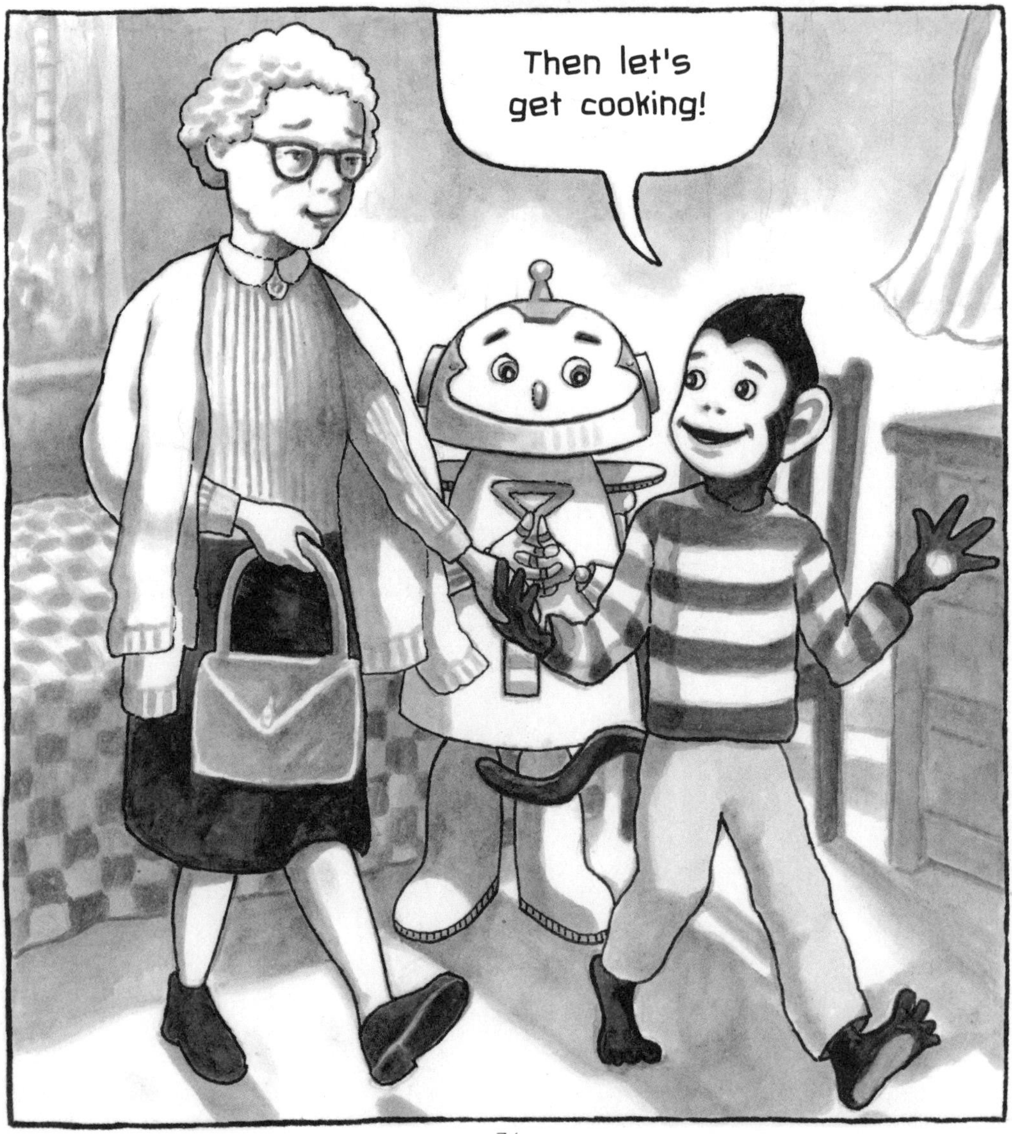
Then let's get cooking!

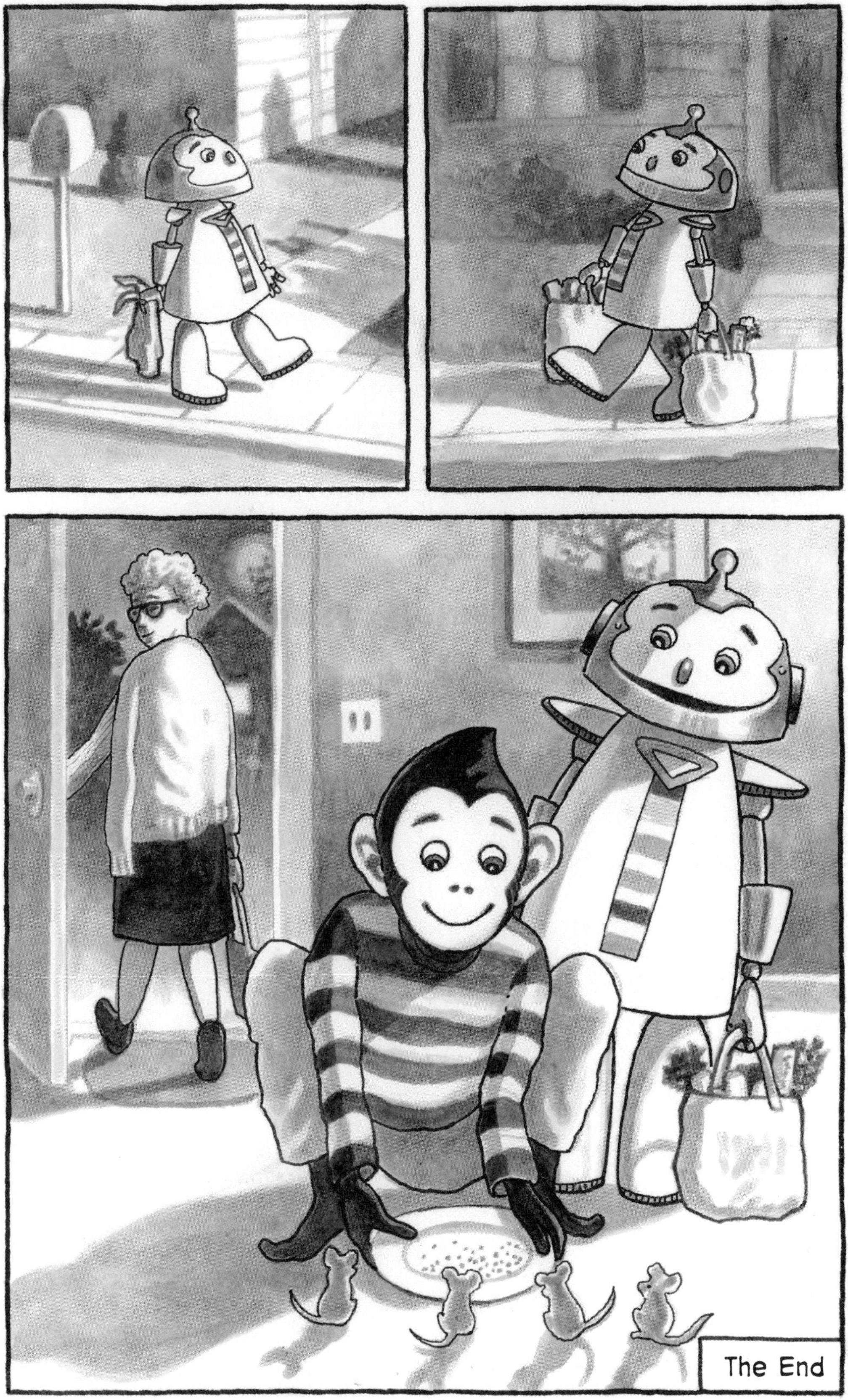
The End

Bird Watchers

Monkey and Robot were babysitting Ms. Harper's parakeet while she was out of town.

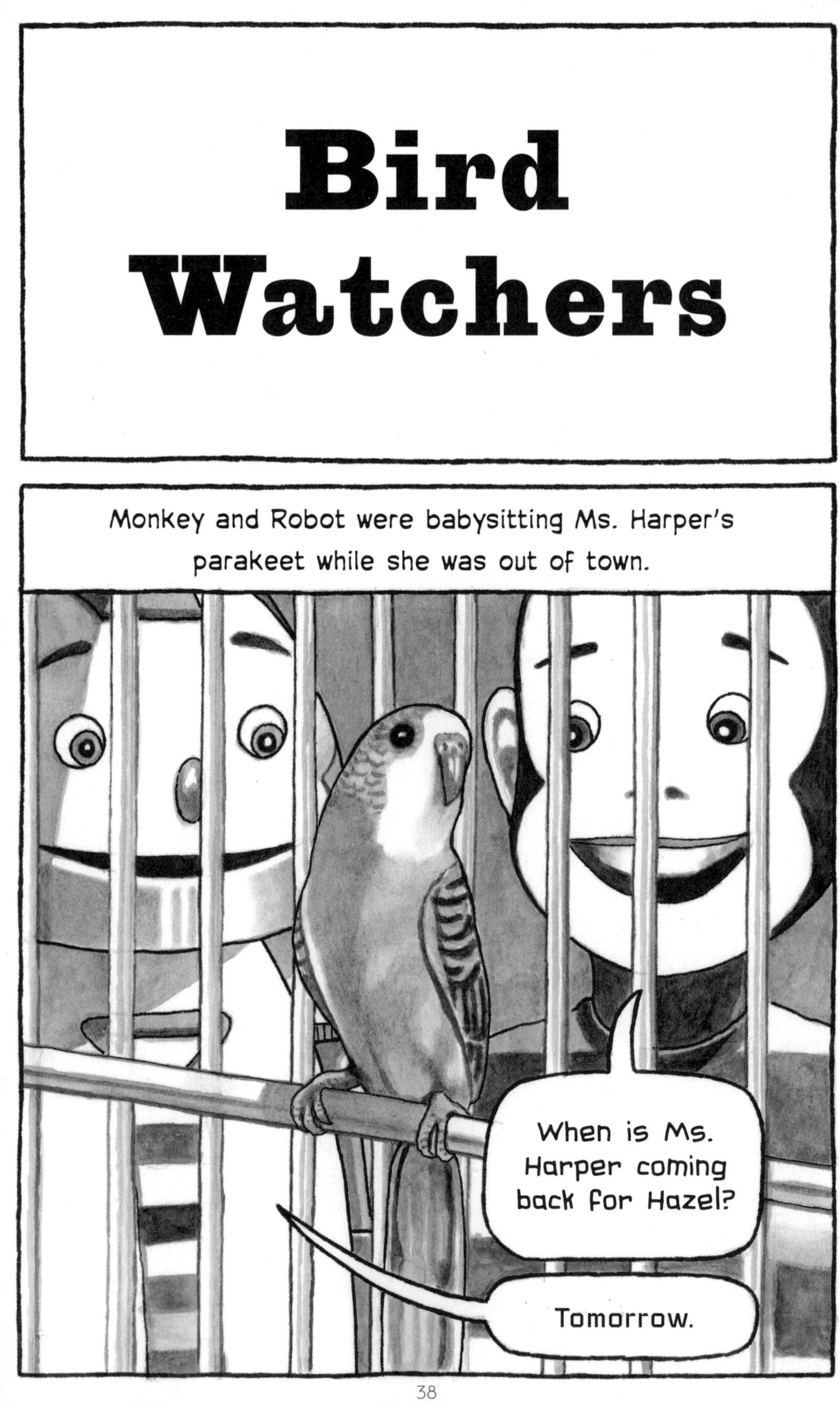
When is Ms. Harper coming back for Hazel?
Tomorrow.

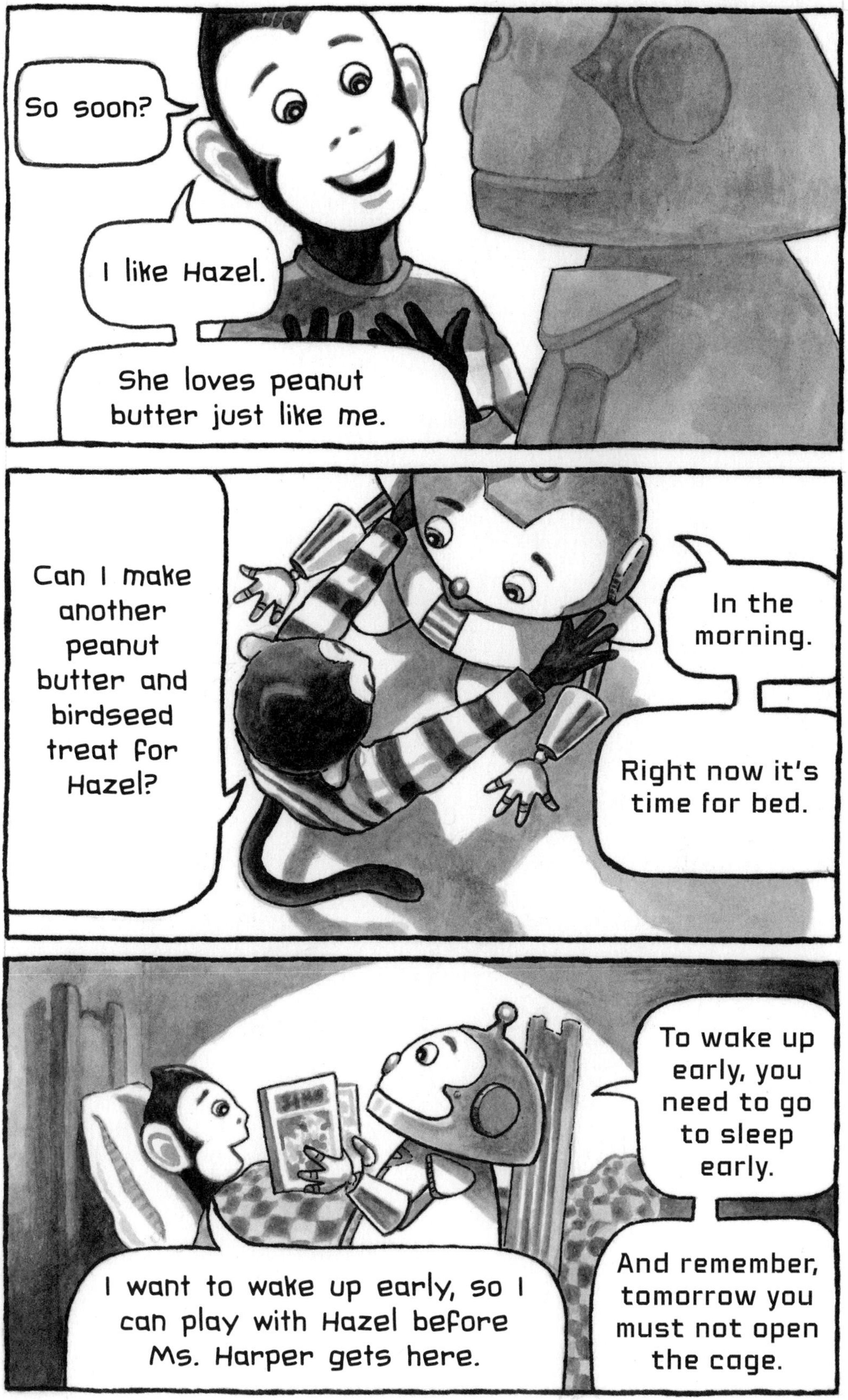

So soon?
I like Hazel.
She loves peanut butter just like me.
Can I make another peanut butter and birdseed treat for Hazel?
In the morning.
Right now it's time for bed.
I want to wake up early, so I can play with Hazel before Ms. Harper gets here.
To wake up early, you need to go to sleep early.
And remember, tomorrow you must not open the cage.

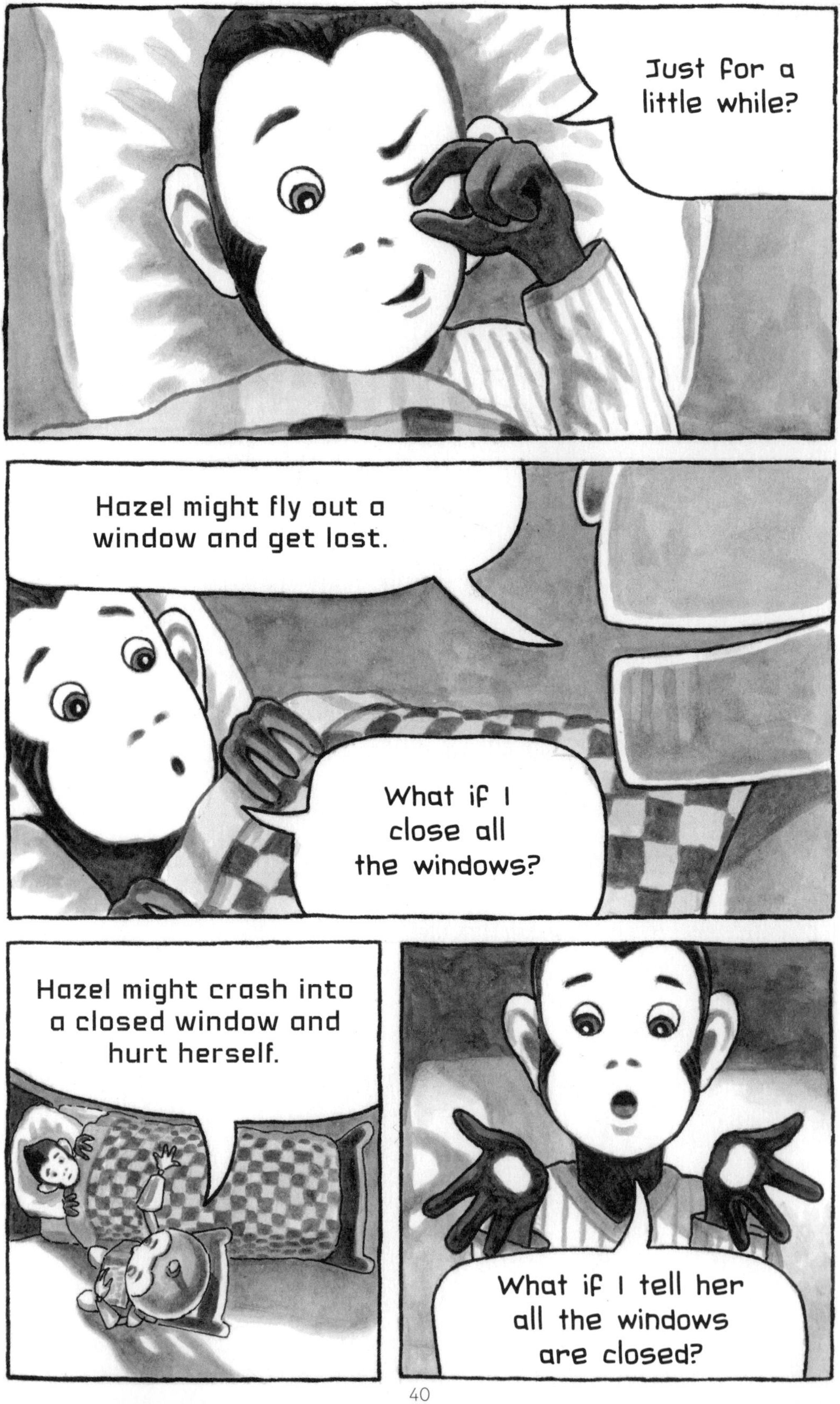
Just for a little while?
Hazel might fly out a window and get lost.
What if I close all the windows?
Hazel might crash into a closed window and hurt herself.
What if I tell her all the windows are closed?

Hazel can't understand you. You don't speak parakeet. Just please don't open the cage.

Robot finished reading the story. Monkey fell asleep. Robot turned off the light and left the room.

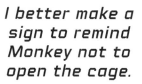

Okay.

I better make a sign to remind Monkey not to open the cage.

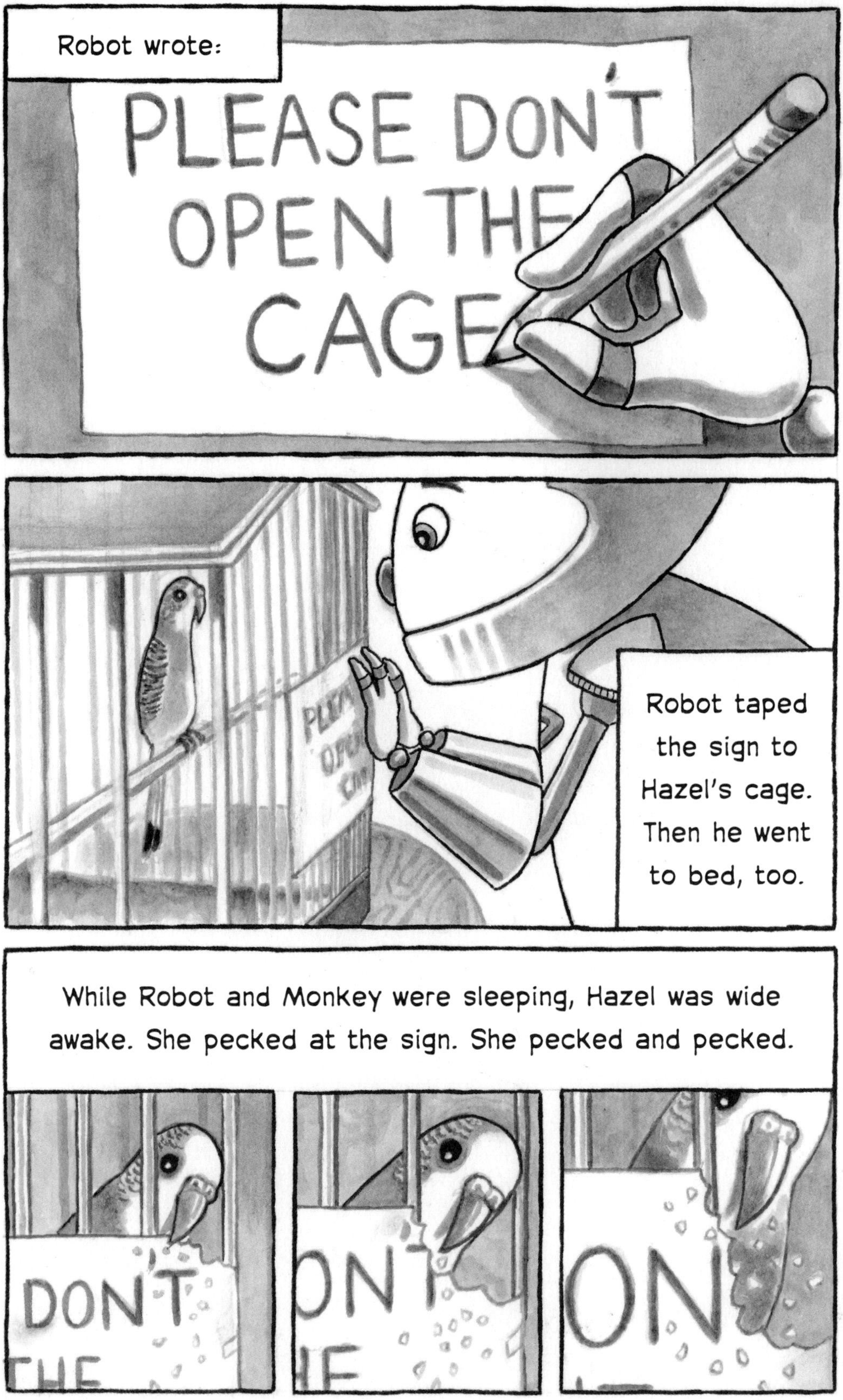
Robot wrote:
PLEASE DON'T OPEN THE CAGE
Robot taped the sign to Hazel's cage. Then he went to bed, too.
While Robot and Monkey were sleeping, Hazel was wide awake. She pecked at the sign. She pecked and pecked.
DON'T

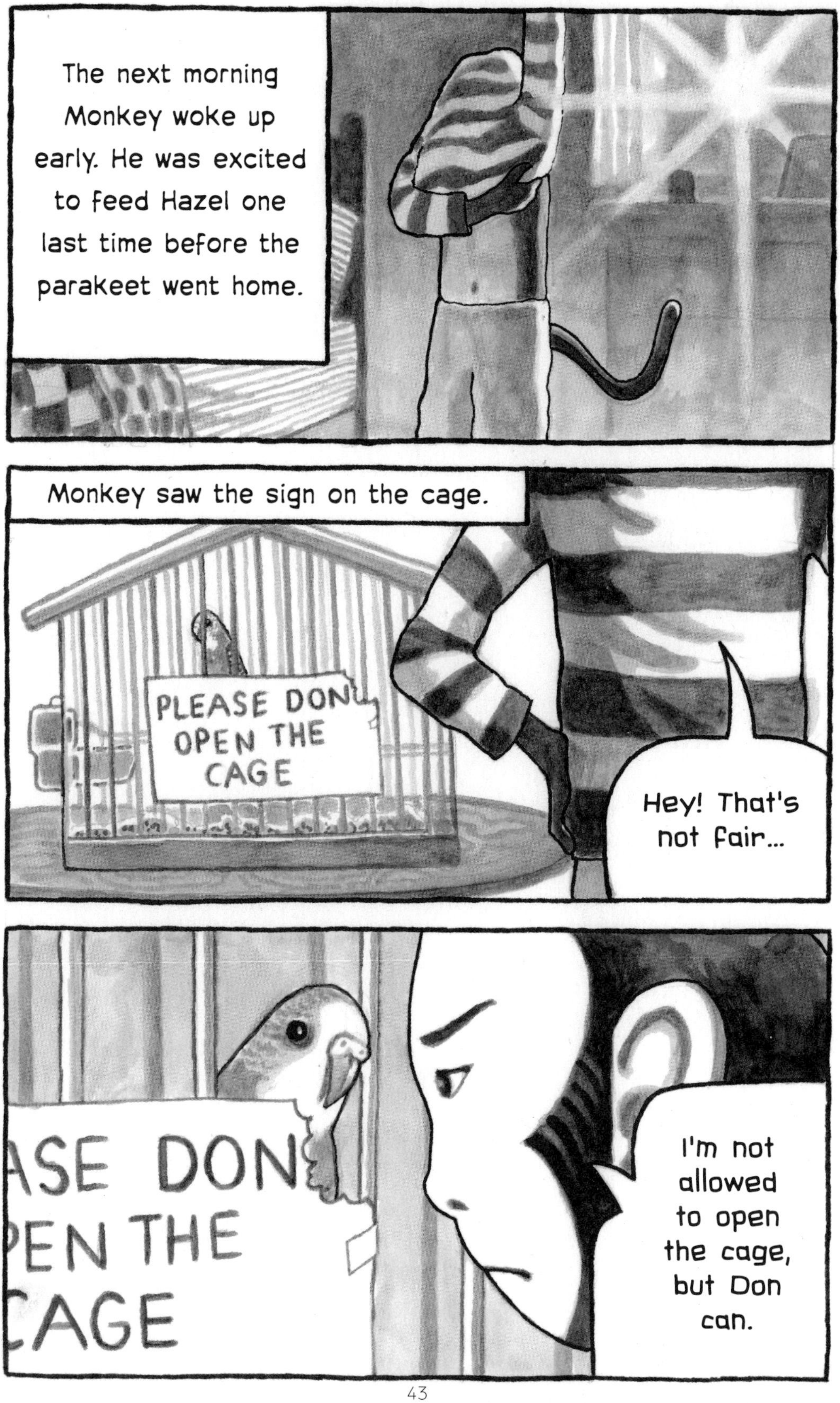
The next morning Monkey woke up early. He was excited to feed Hazel one last time before the parakeet went home.
Monkey saw the sign on the cage.
PLEASE DON OPEN THE CAGE
Hey! That's not fair...
ASE DON
PEN THE
CAGE
I'm not allowed to open the cage, but Don can.

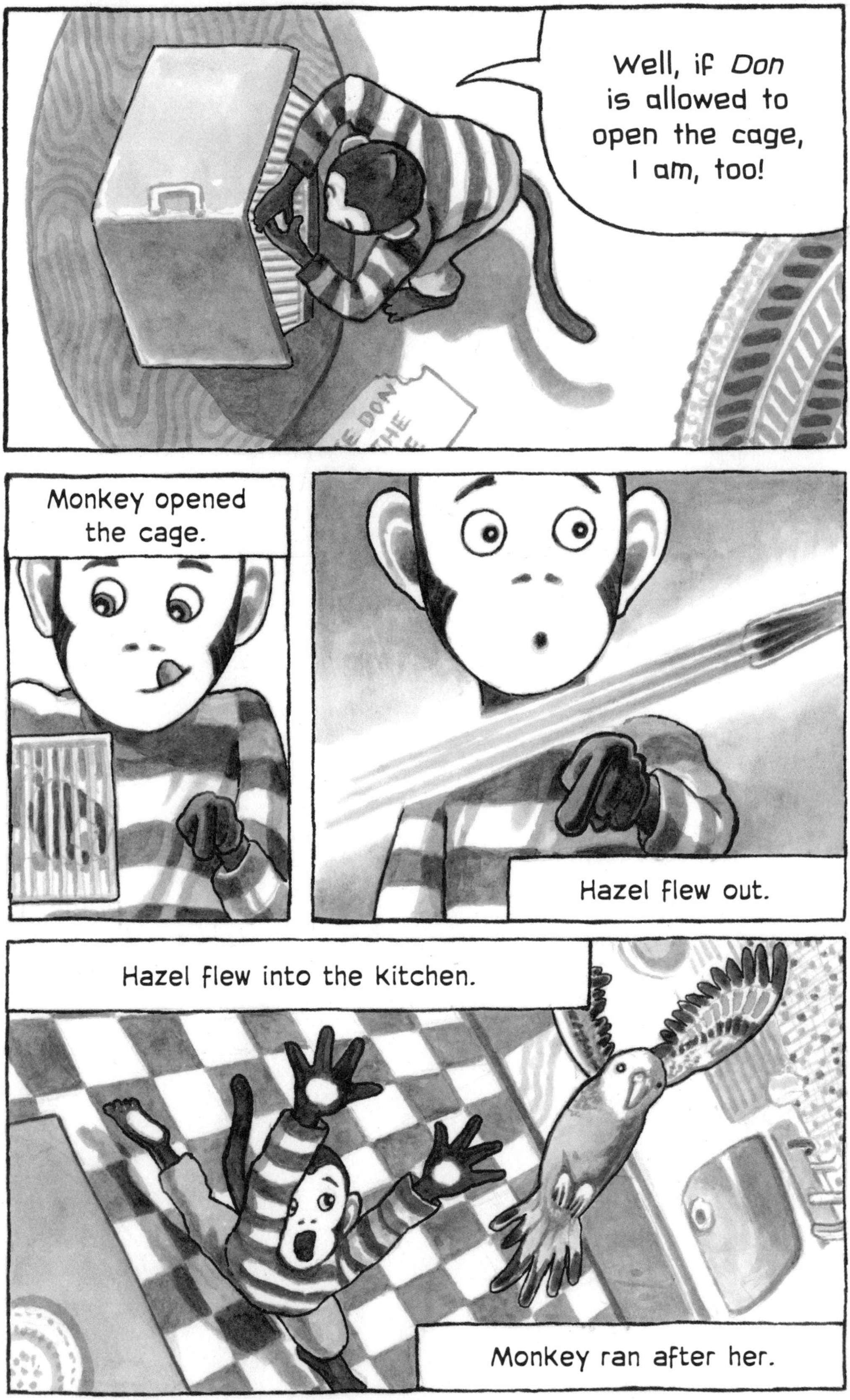
Well, if *Don* is allowed to open the cage, I am, too!
Monkey opened the cage.
Hazel flew out.
Hazel flew into the kitchen.
Monkey ran after her.

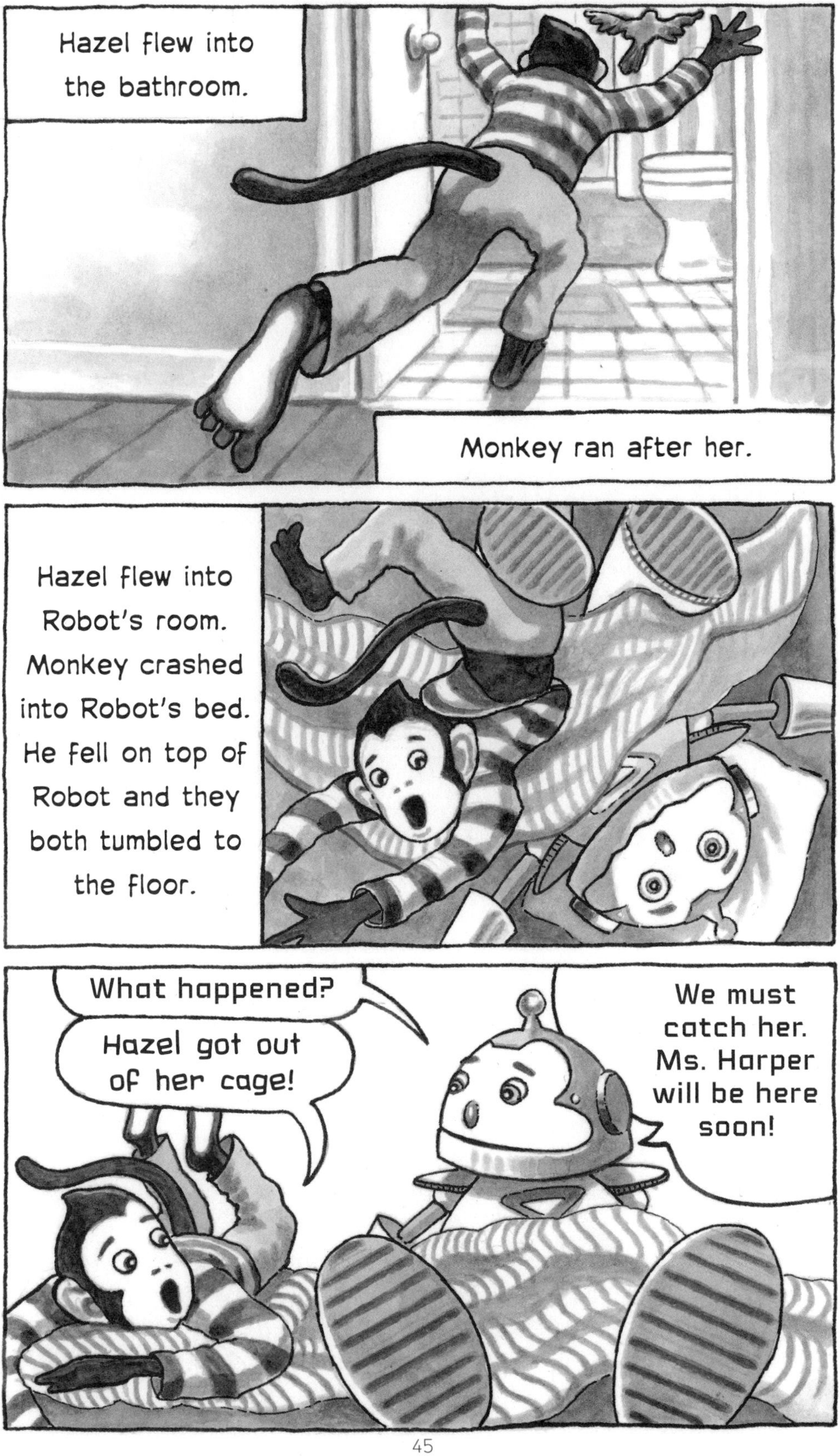
Hazel flew into the bathroom.
Monkey ran after her.
Hazel flew into Robot's room. Monkey crashed into Robot's bed. He fell on top of Robot and they both tumbled to the floor.
What happened?
Hazel got out of her cage!
We must catch her. Ms. Harper will be here soon!

Monkey and Robot ran to the kitchen. They didn't see Hazel. They looked in the bathroom, the living room, and both bedrooms. The window in Monkey's room was wide open.

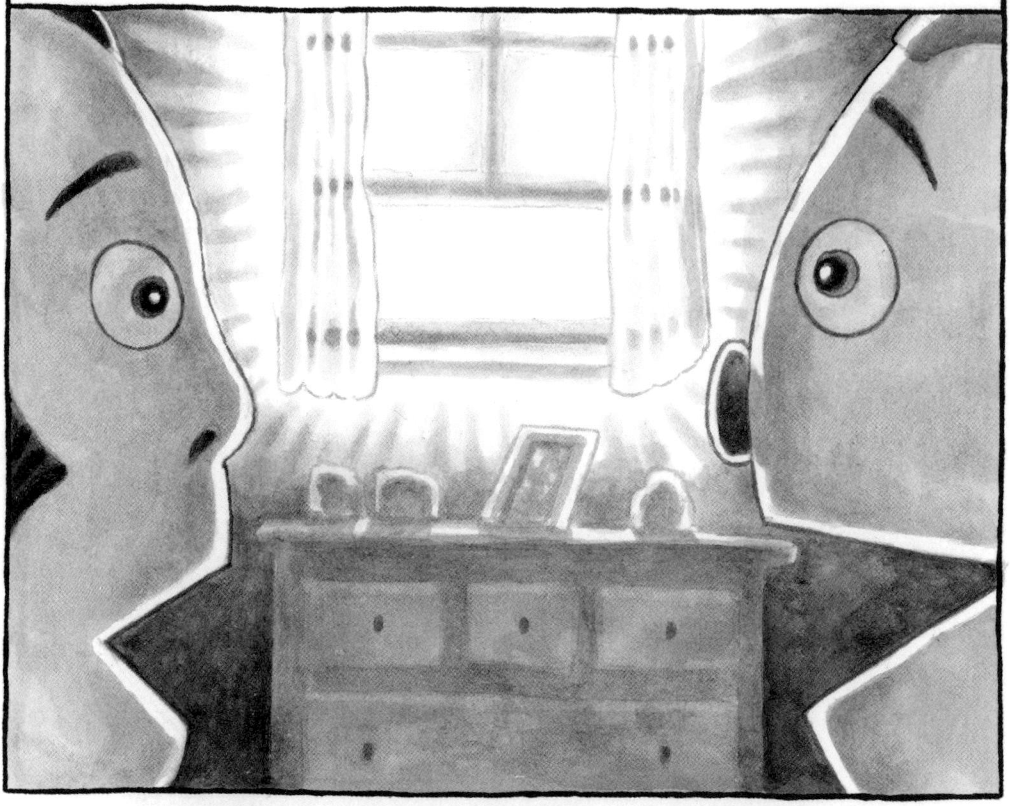

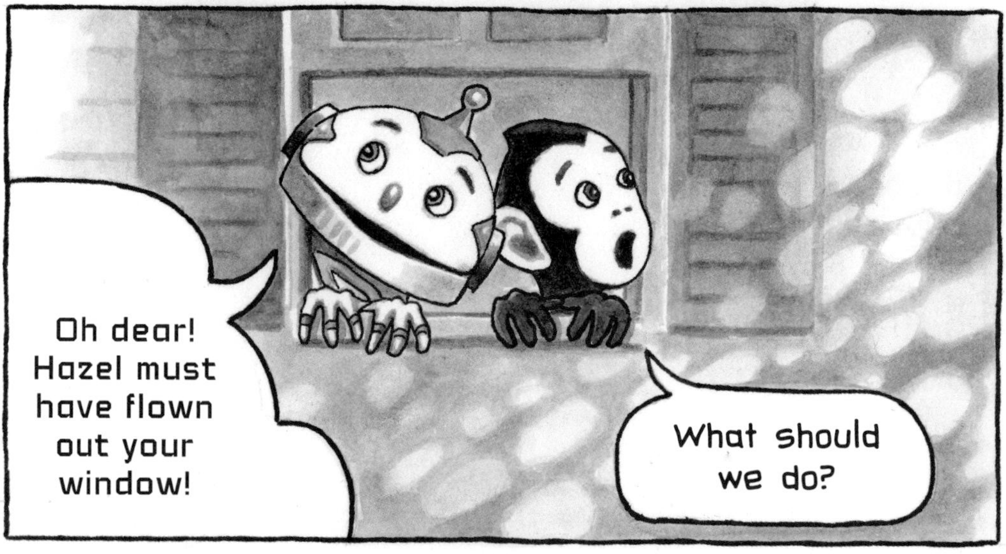
Oh dear! Hazel must have flown out your window!
What should we do?

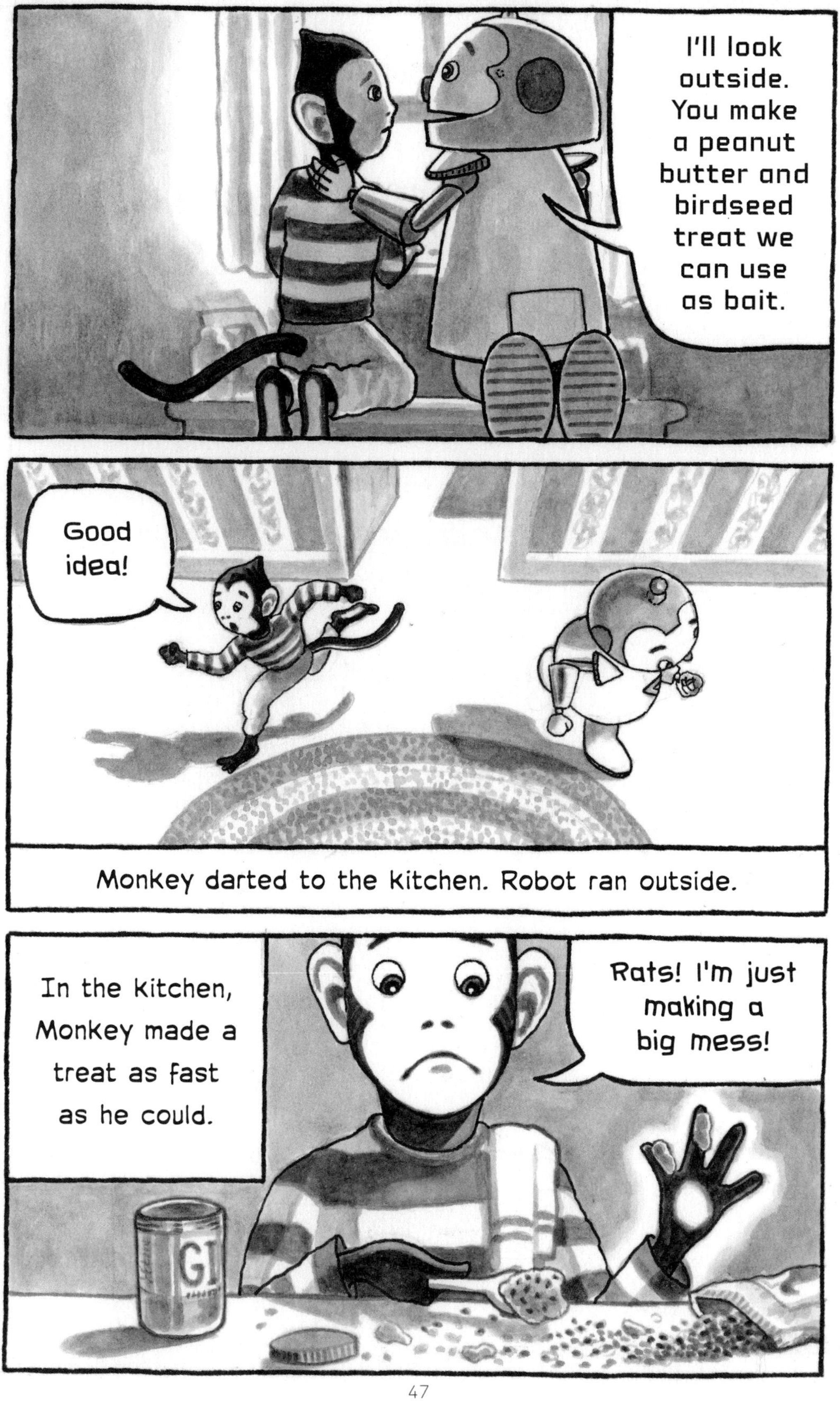
I'll look outside. You make a peanut butter and birdseed treat we can use as bait.
Good idea!
Monkey darted to the kitchen. Robot ran outside.
In the kitchen, Monkey made a treat as fast as he could.
Rats! I'm just making a big mess!

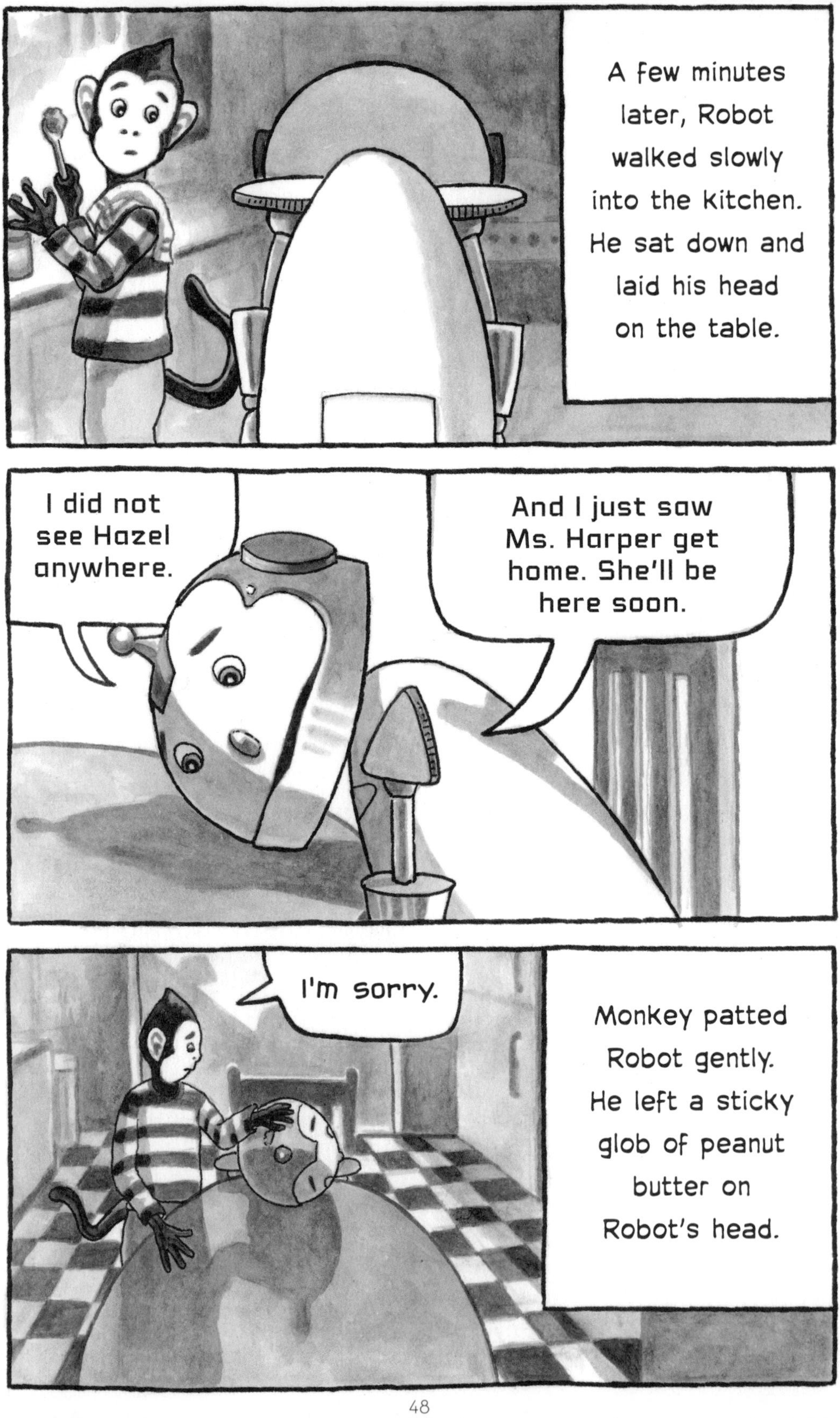
A few minutes later, Robot walked slowly into the kitchen. He sat down and laid his head on the table.
I did not see Hazel anywhere.
And I just saw Ms. Harper get home. She'll be here soon.
I'm sorry.
Monkey patted Robot gently. He left a sticky glob of peanut butter on Robot's head.

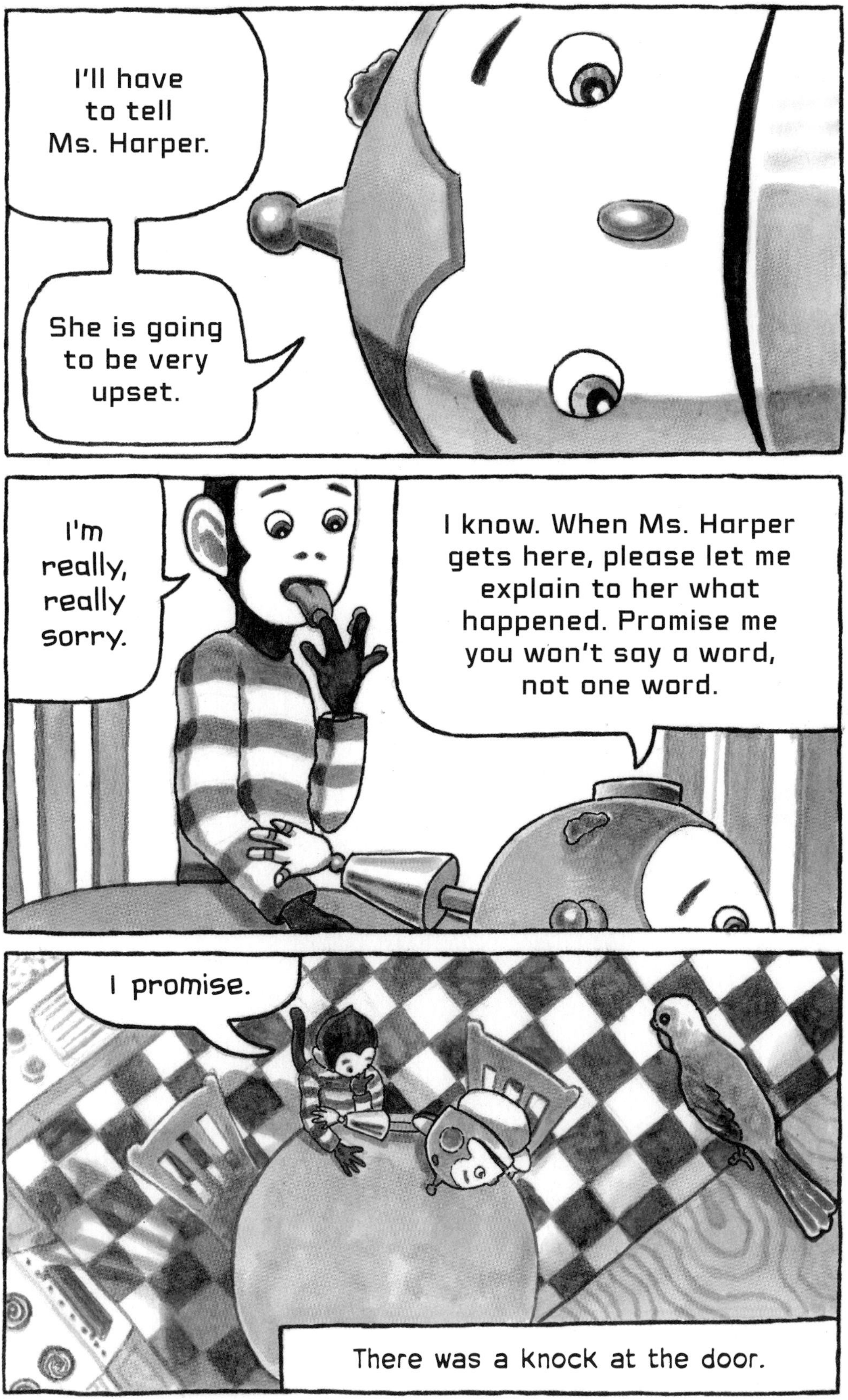
I'll have to tell Ms. Harper.
She is going to be very upset.
I'm really, really sorry.
I know. When Ms. Harper gets here, please let me explain to her what happened. Promise me you won't say a word, not one word.
I promise.
There was a knock at the door.

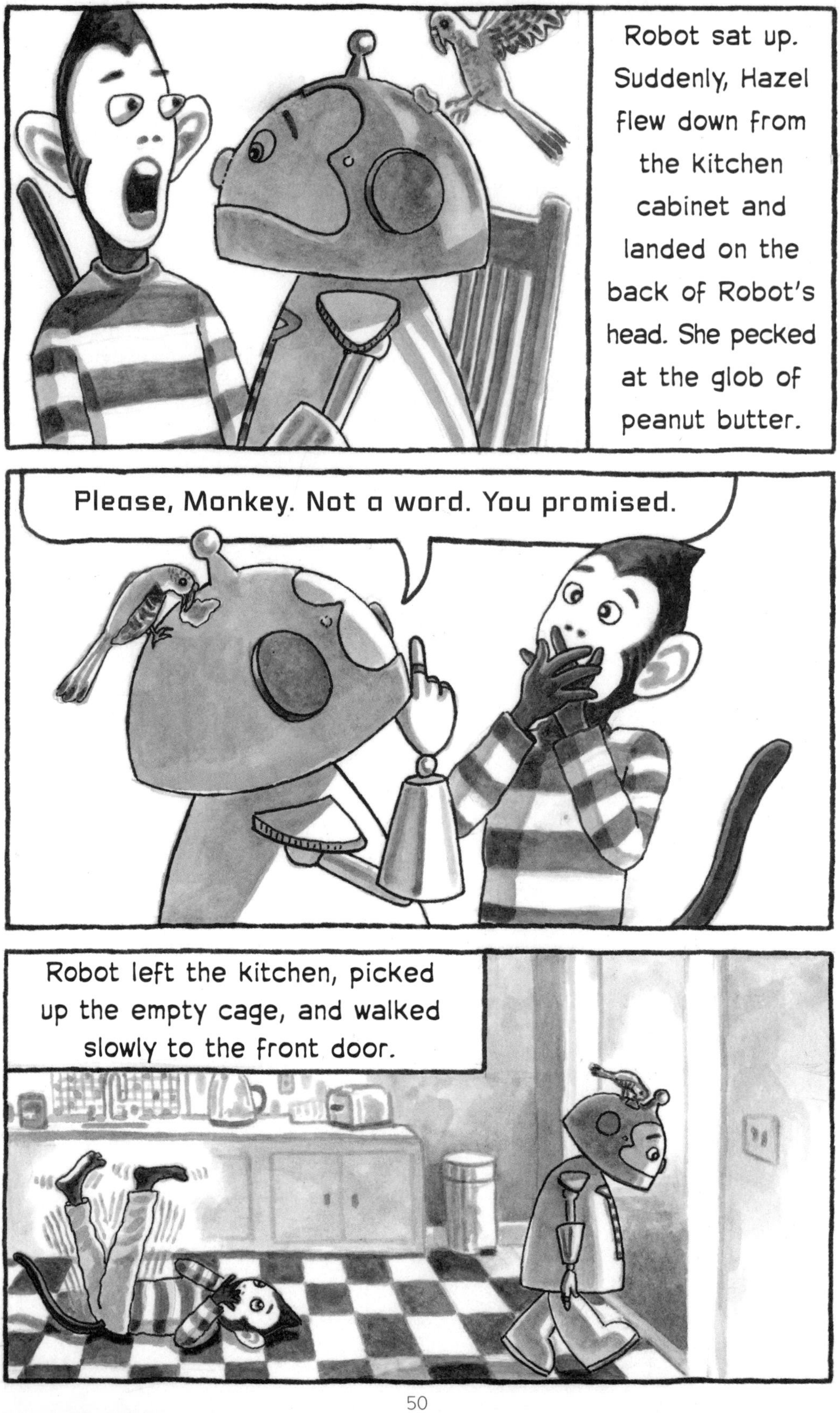
Robot sat up. Suddenly, Hazel flew down from the kitchen cabinet and landed on the back of Robot's head. She pecked at the glob of peanut butter.
Please, Monkey. Not a word. You promised.
Robot left the kitchen, picked up the empty cage, and walked slowly to the front door.

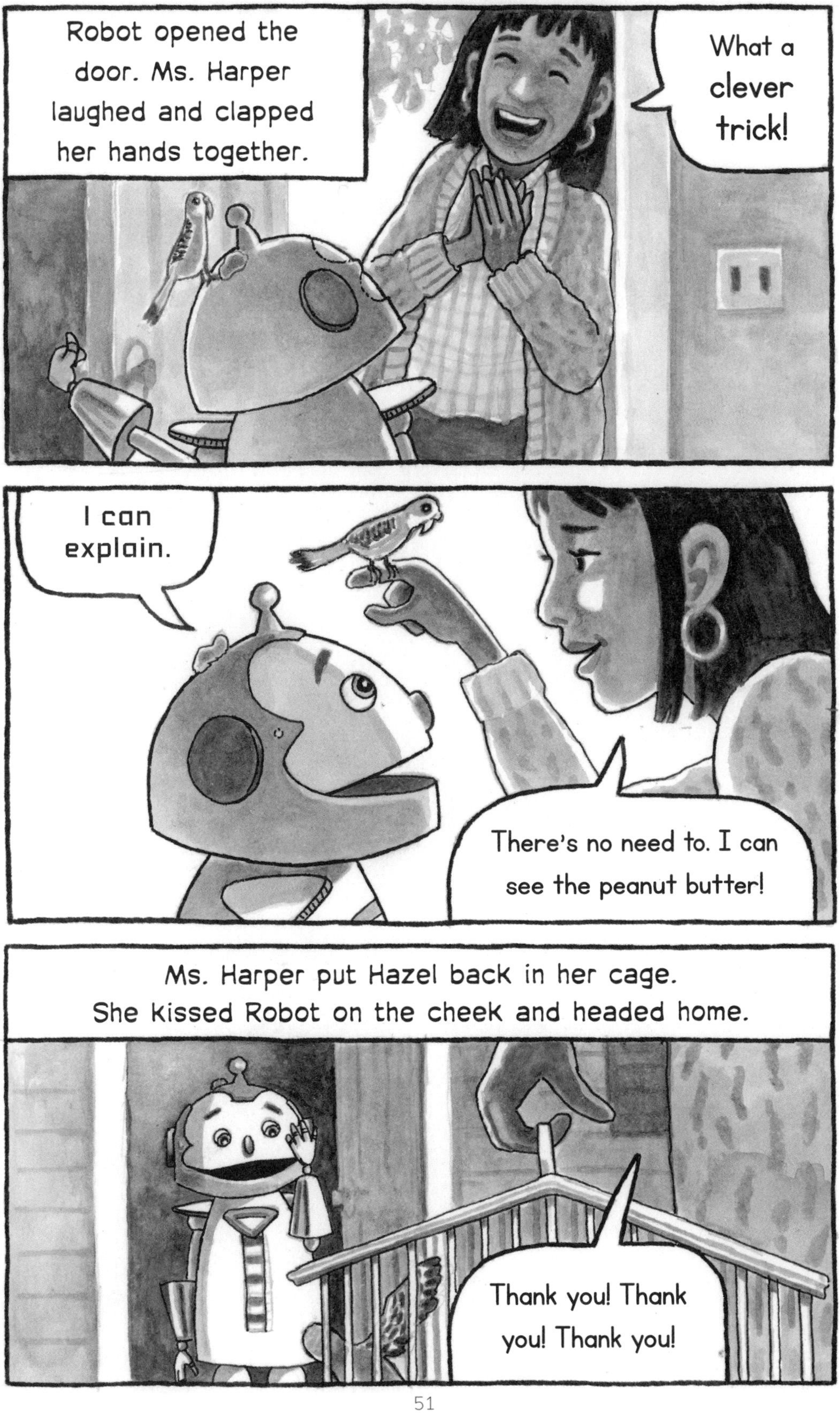
Robot opened the door. Ms. Harper laughed and clapped her hands together.
What a clever trick!
I can explain.
There's no need to. I can see the peanut butter!
Ms. Harper put Hazel back in her cage. She kissed Robot on the cheek and headed home.
Thank you! Thank you! Thank you!

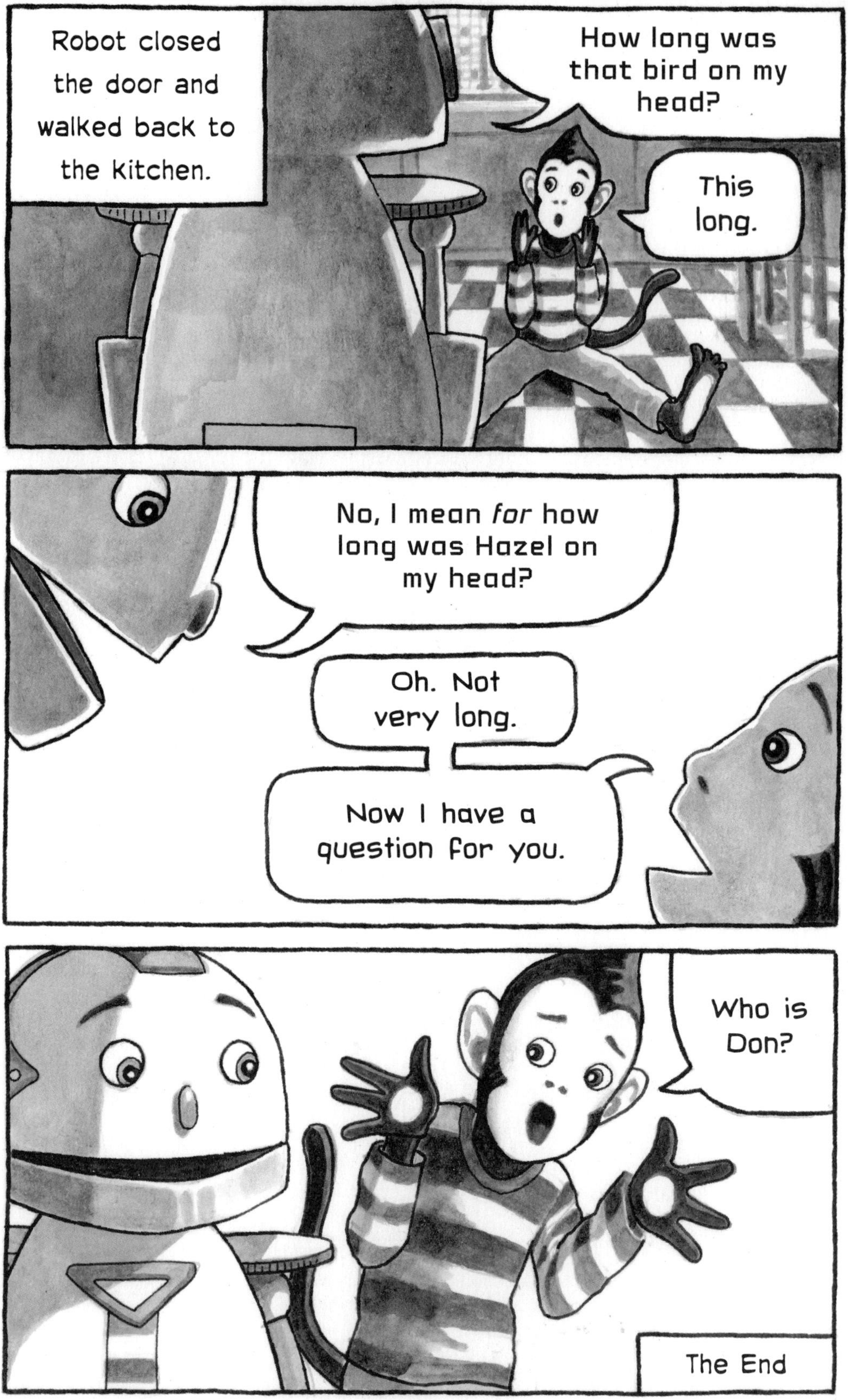
Robot closed the door and walked back to the kitchen.
How long was that bird on my head?
This long.
No, I mean *for* how long was Hazel on my head?
Oh. Not very long.
Now I have a question for you.
Who is Don?
The End

Monkey See, Monkey Don't!

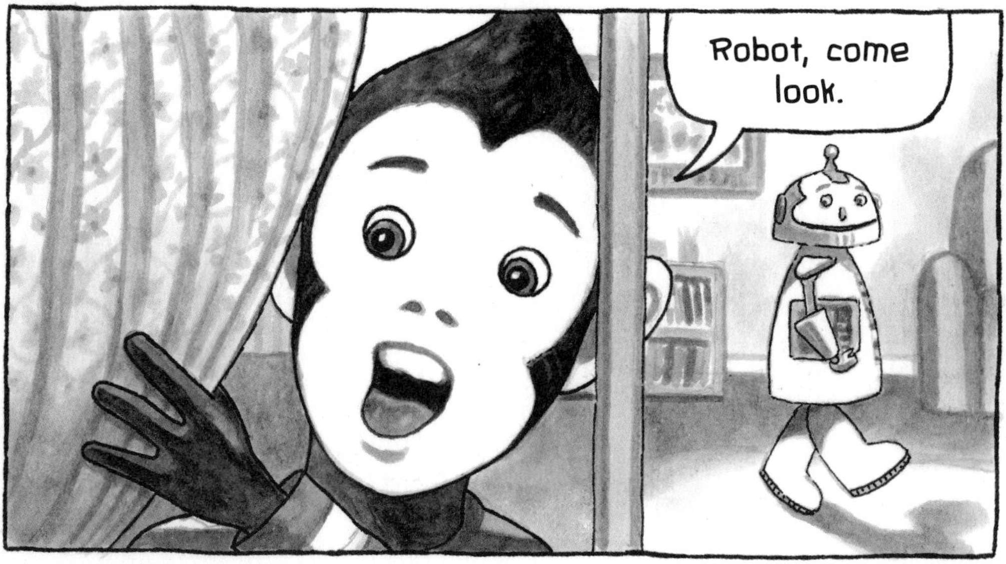
Robot, come look.

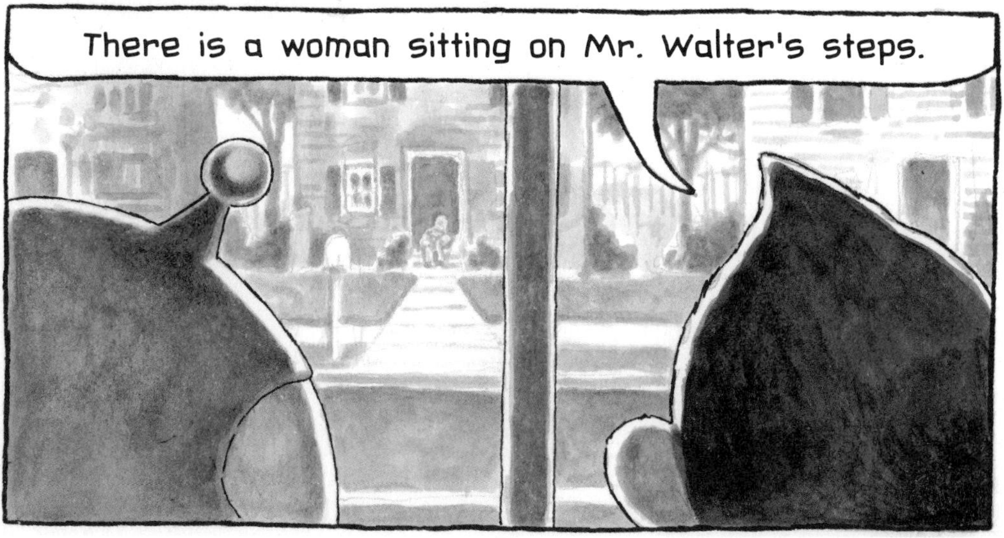
There is a woman sitting on Mr. Walter's steps.

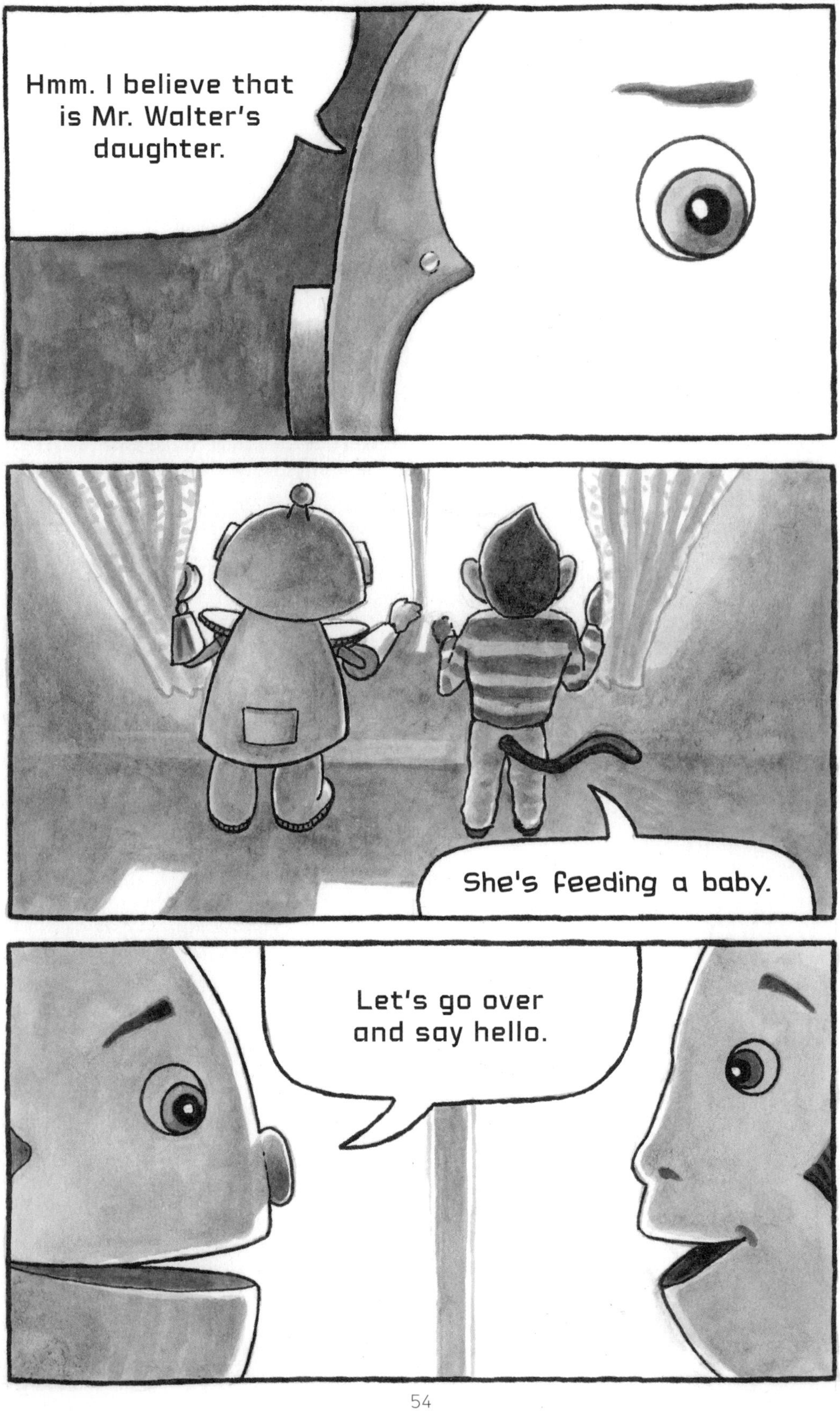
Hmm. I believe that is Mr. Walter's daughter.
She's feeding a baby.
Let's go over and say hello.

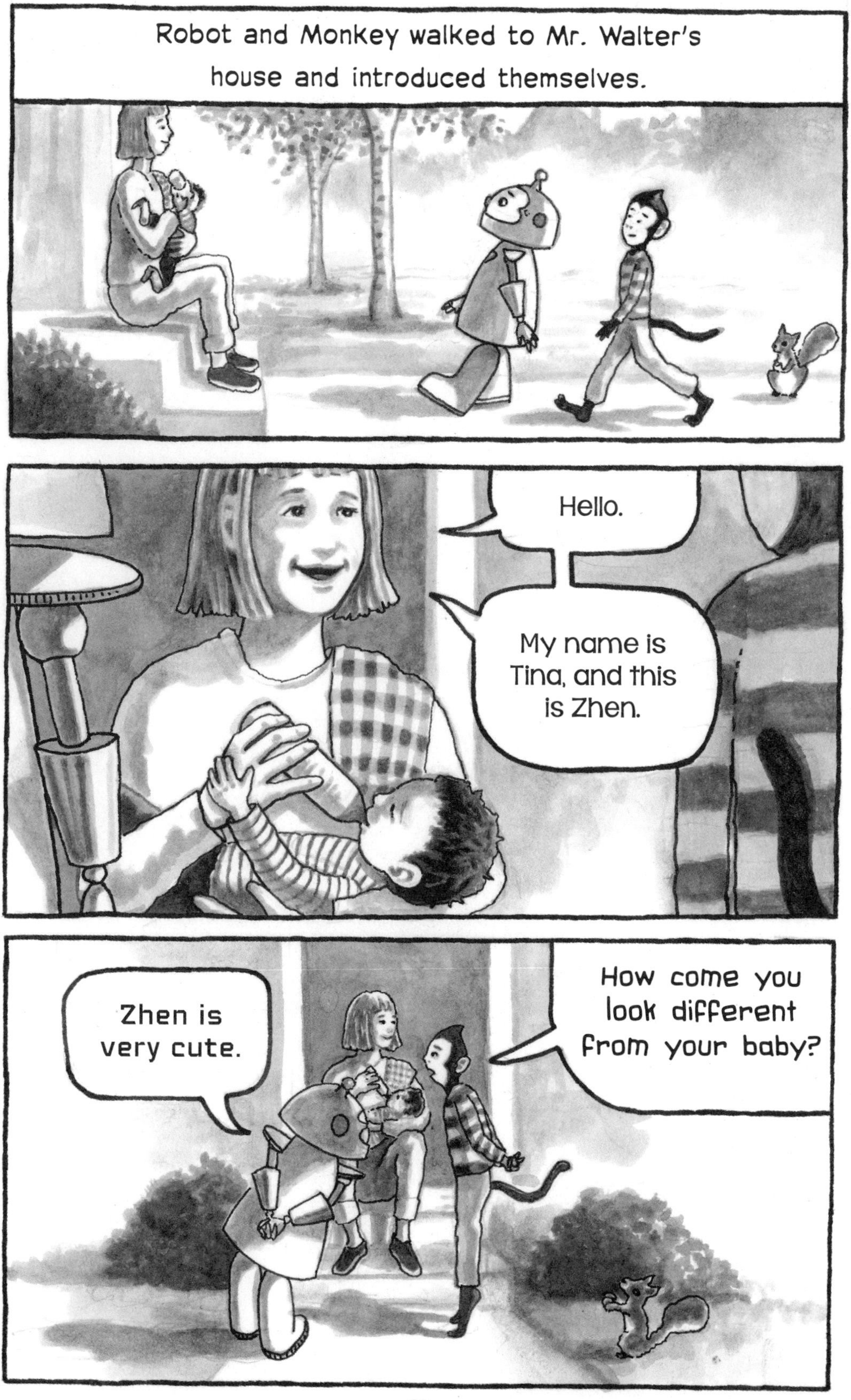
Robot and Monkey walked to Mr. Walter's house and introduced themselves.
Hello.
My name is Tina, and this is Zhen.
Zhen is very cute.
How come you look different from your baby?

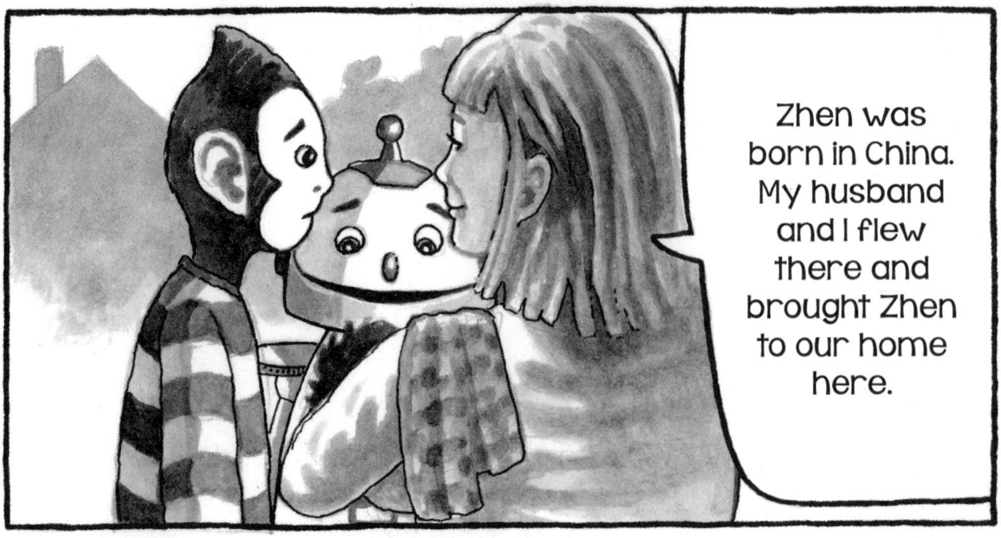
Zhen was born in China. My husband and I flew there and brought Zhen to our home here.

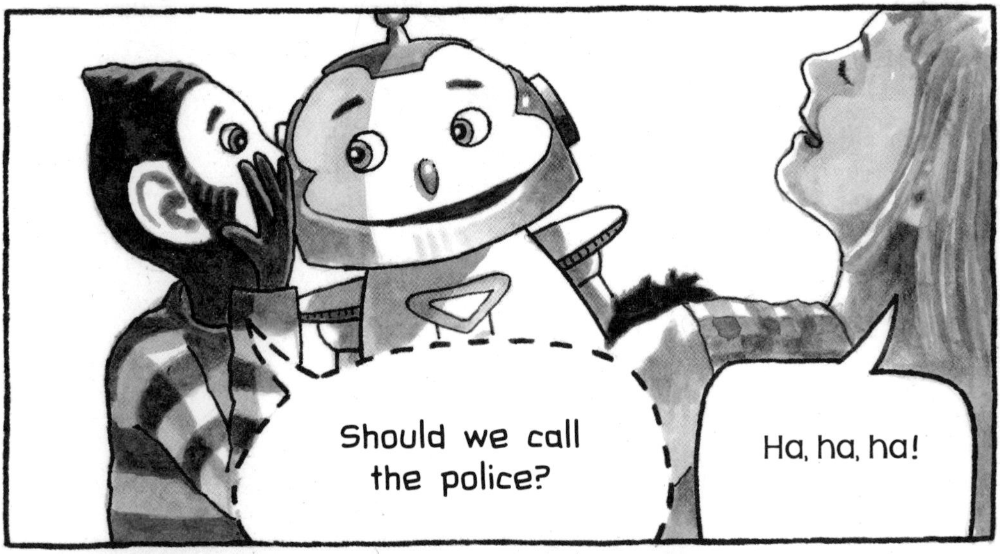
Should we call the police?
Ha, ha, ha!

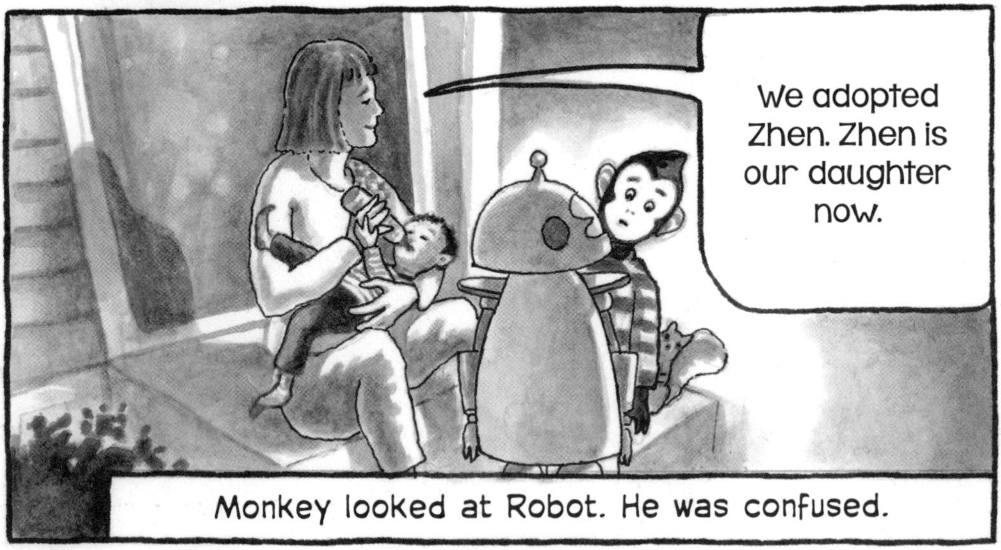
We adopted Zhen. Zhen is our daughter now.
Monkey looked at Robot. He was confused.

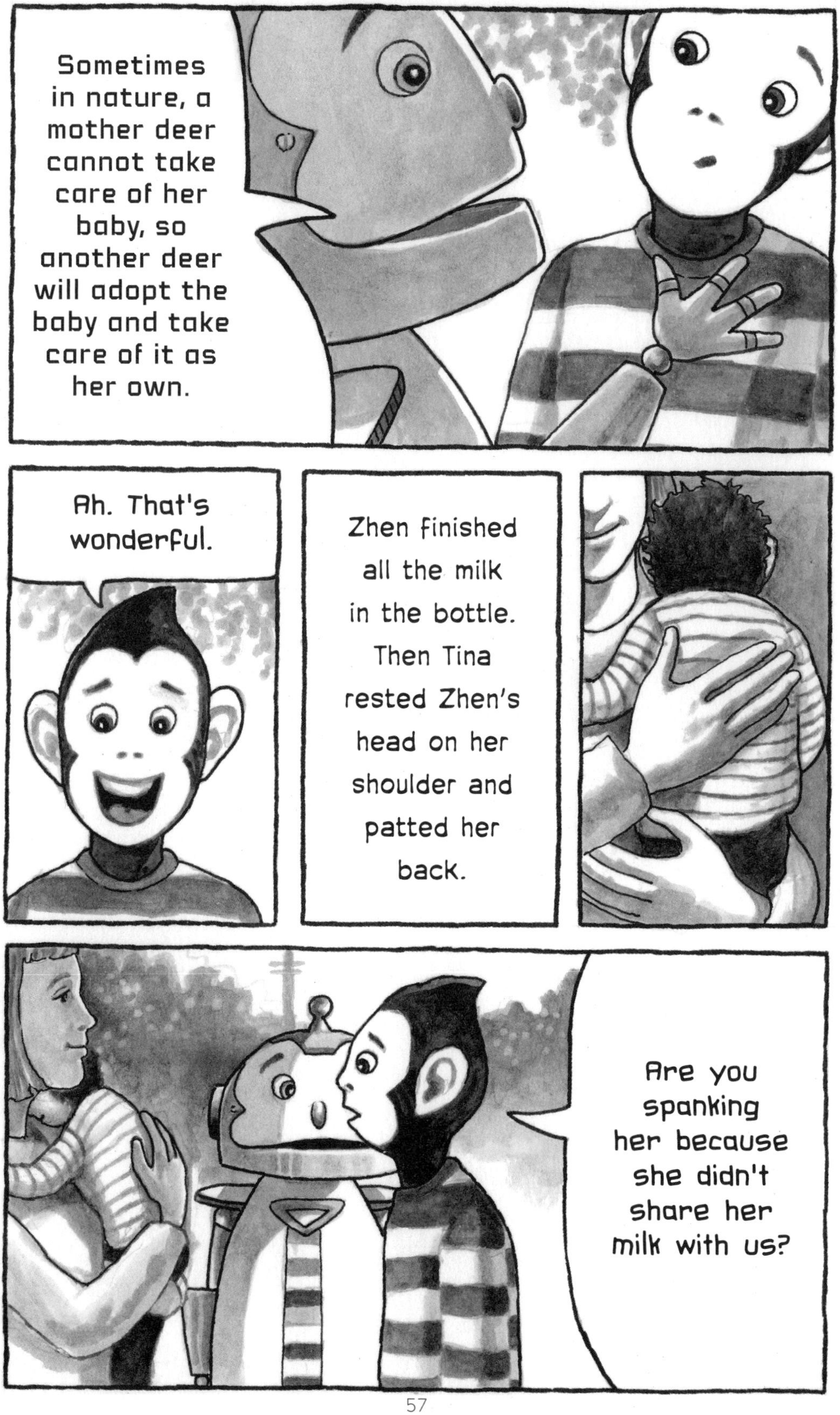
Sometimes in nature, a mother deer cannot take care of her baby, so another deer will adopt the baby and take care of it as her own.
Ah. That's wonderful.
Zhen finished all the milk in the bottle. Then Tina rested Zhen's head on her shoulder and patted her back.
Are you spanking her because she didn't share her milk with us?

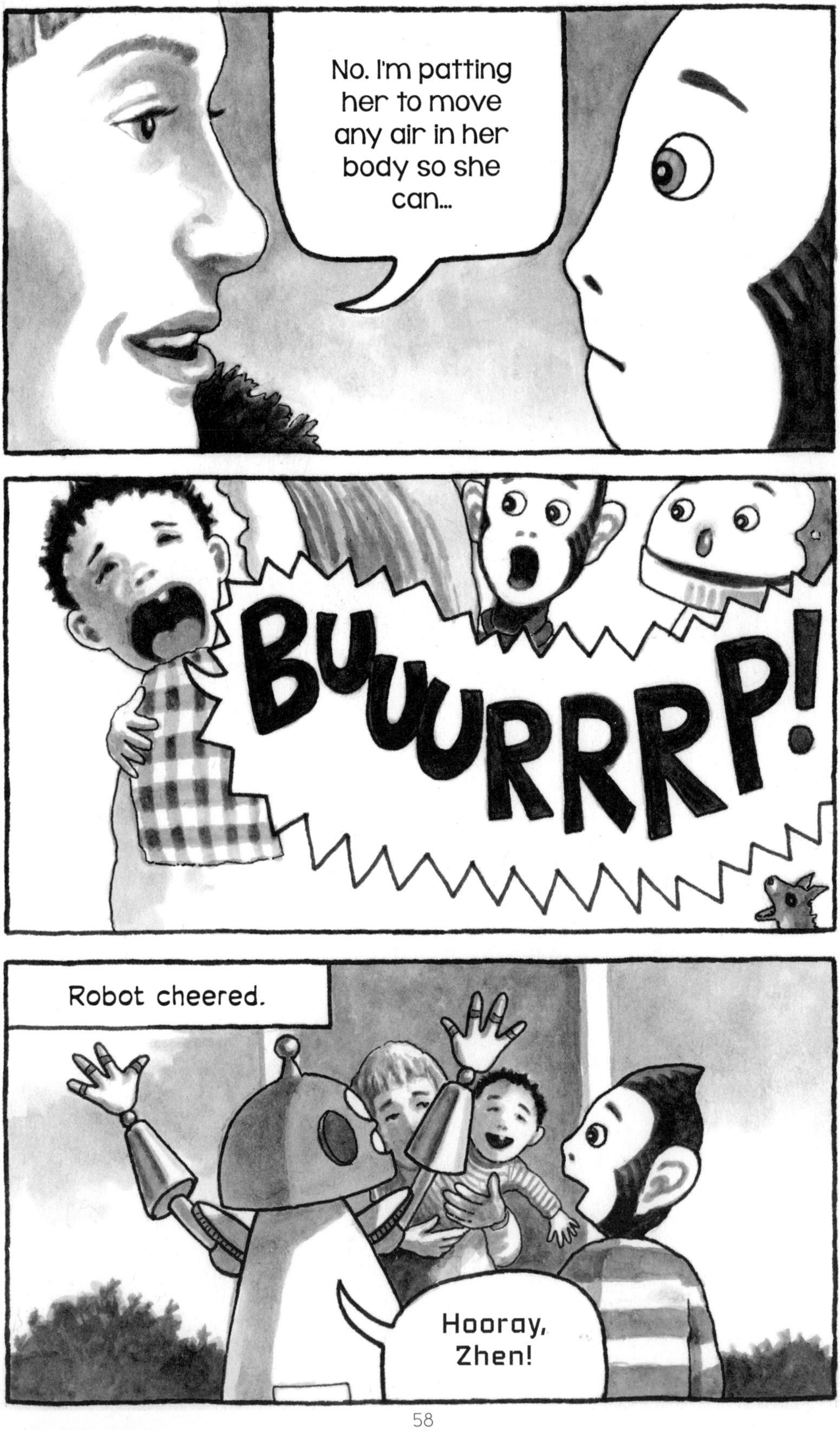
No. I'm patting her to move any air in her body so she can...
BUUURRRP!
Robot cheered.
Hooray, Zhen!

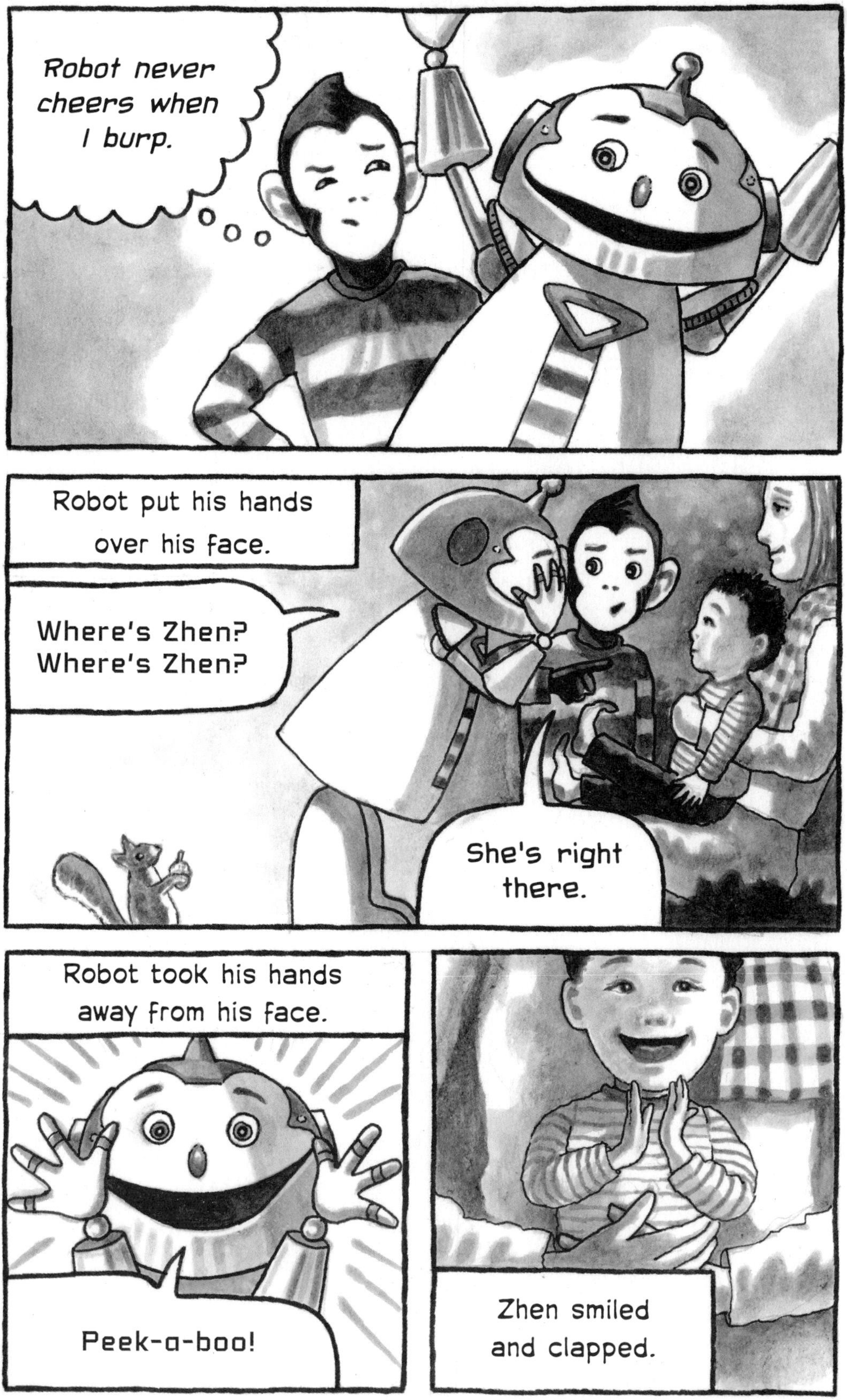
Robot never cheers when I burp.
Robot put his hands over his face.
Where's Zhen? Where's Zhen?
She's right there.
Robot took his hands away from his face.
Peek-a-boo!
Zhen smiled and clapped.

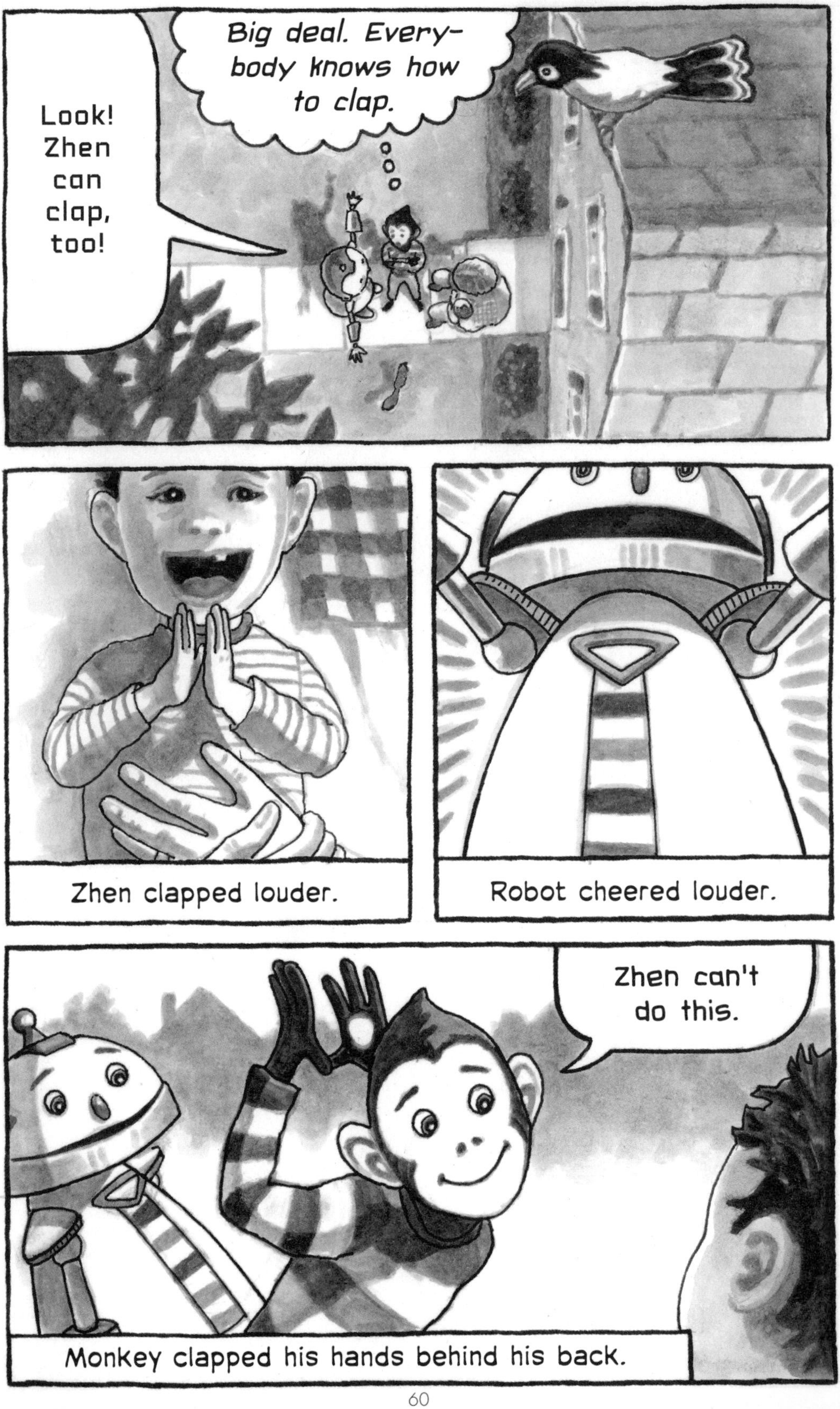
Look! Zhen can clap, too!
Big deal. Every-body knows how to clap.
Zhen clapped louder.
Robot cheered louder.
Zhen can't do this.
Monkey clapped his hands behind his back.

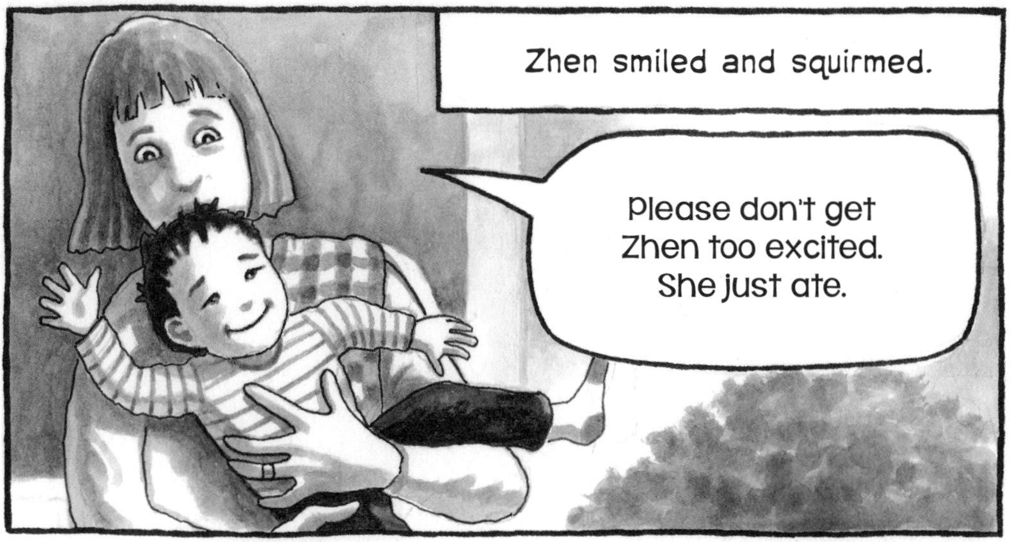
Zhen smiled and squirmed.
Please don't get Zhen too excited. She just ate.

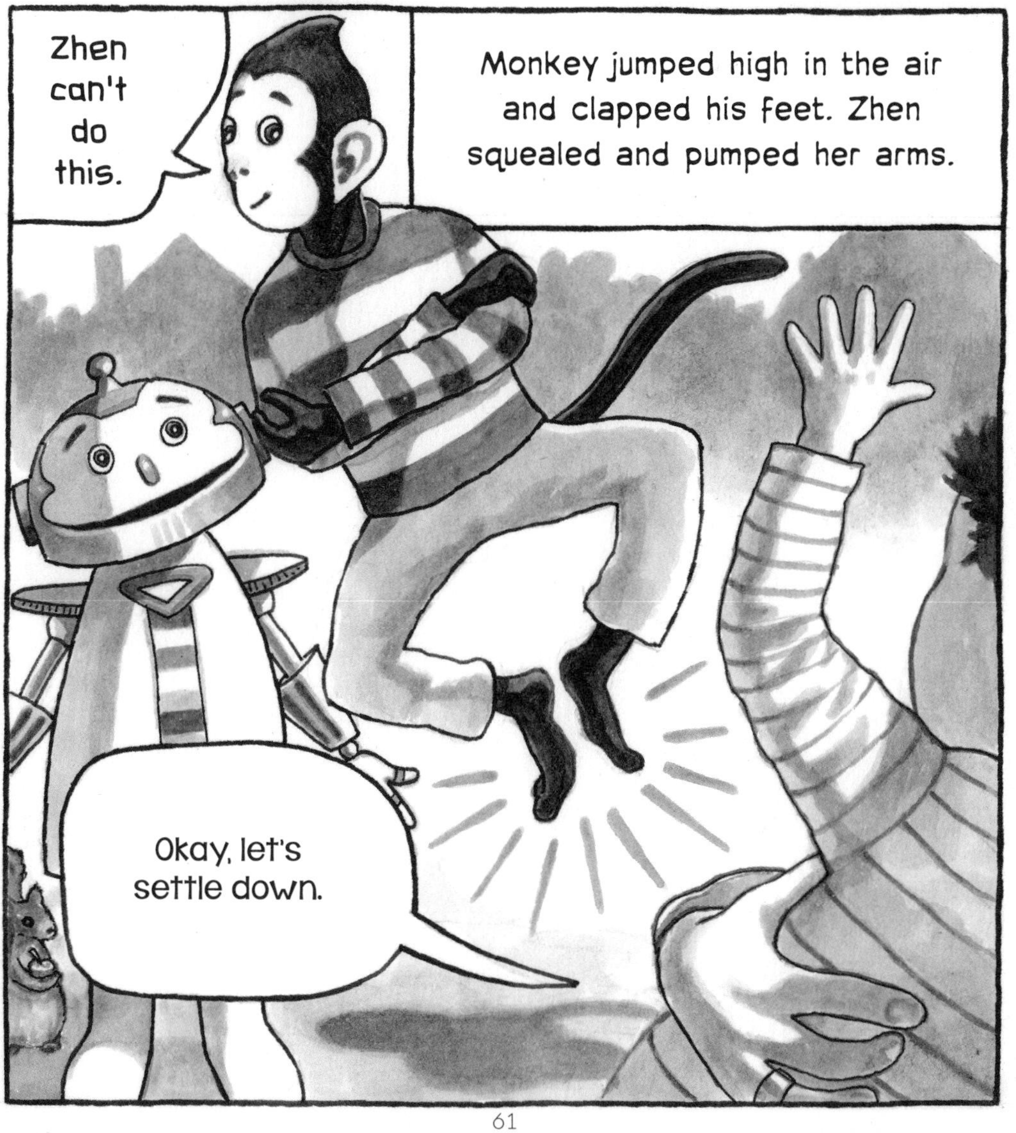
Monkey jumped high in the air and clapped his feet. Zhen squealed and pumped her arms.
Zhen can't do this.
Okay, let's settle down.

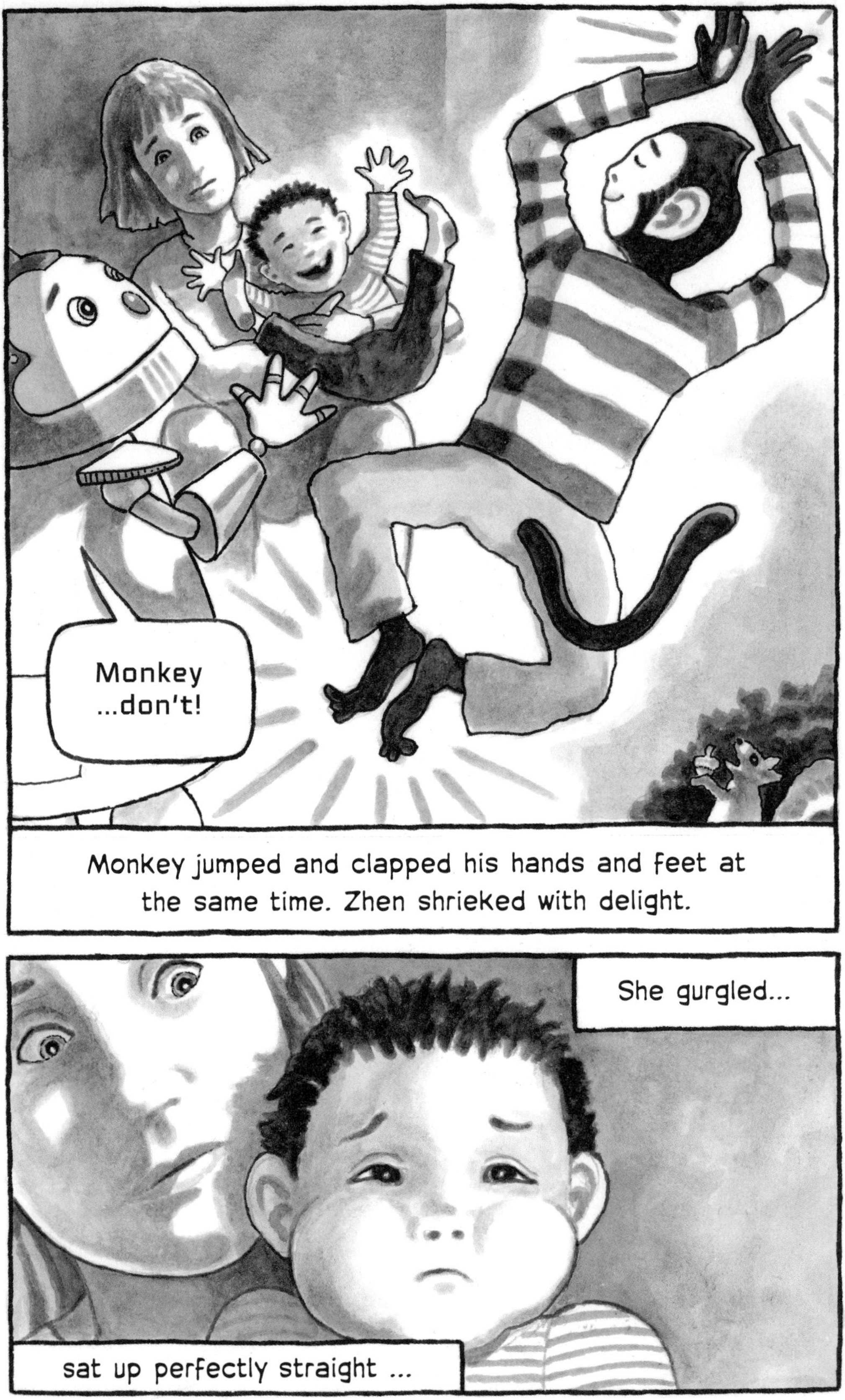
Monkey
...don't!
Monkey jumped and clapped his hands and feet at the same time. Zhen shrieked with delight.
She gurgled...
sat up perfectly straight ...

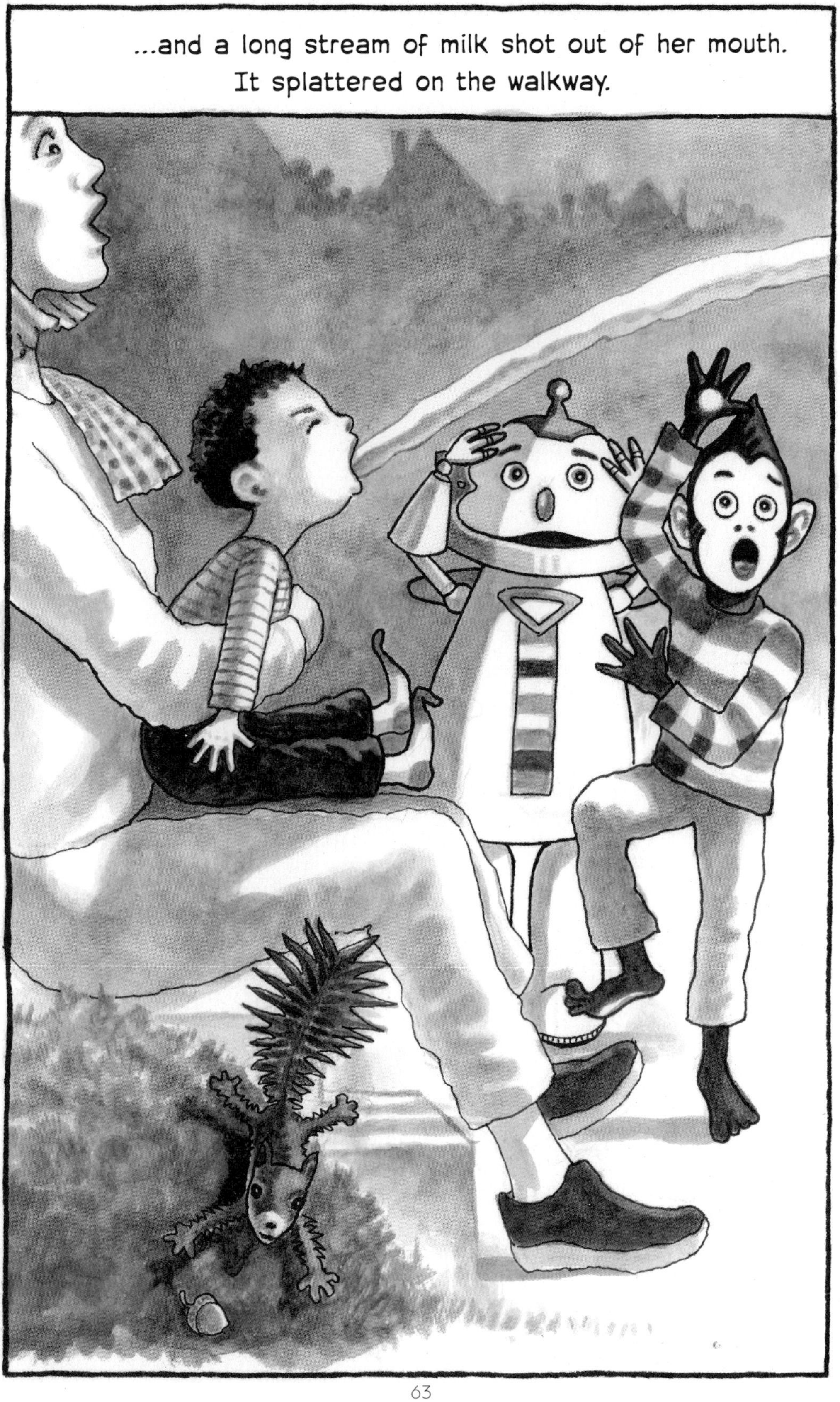
...and a long stream of milk shot out of her mouth.
It splattered on the walkway.

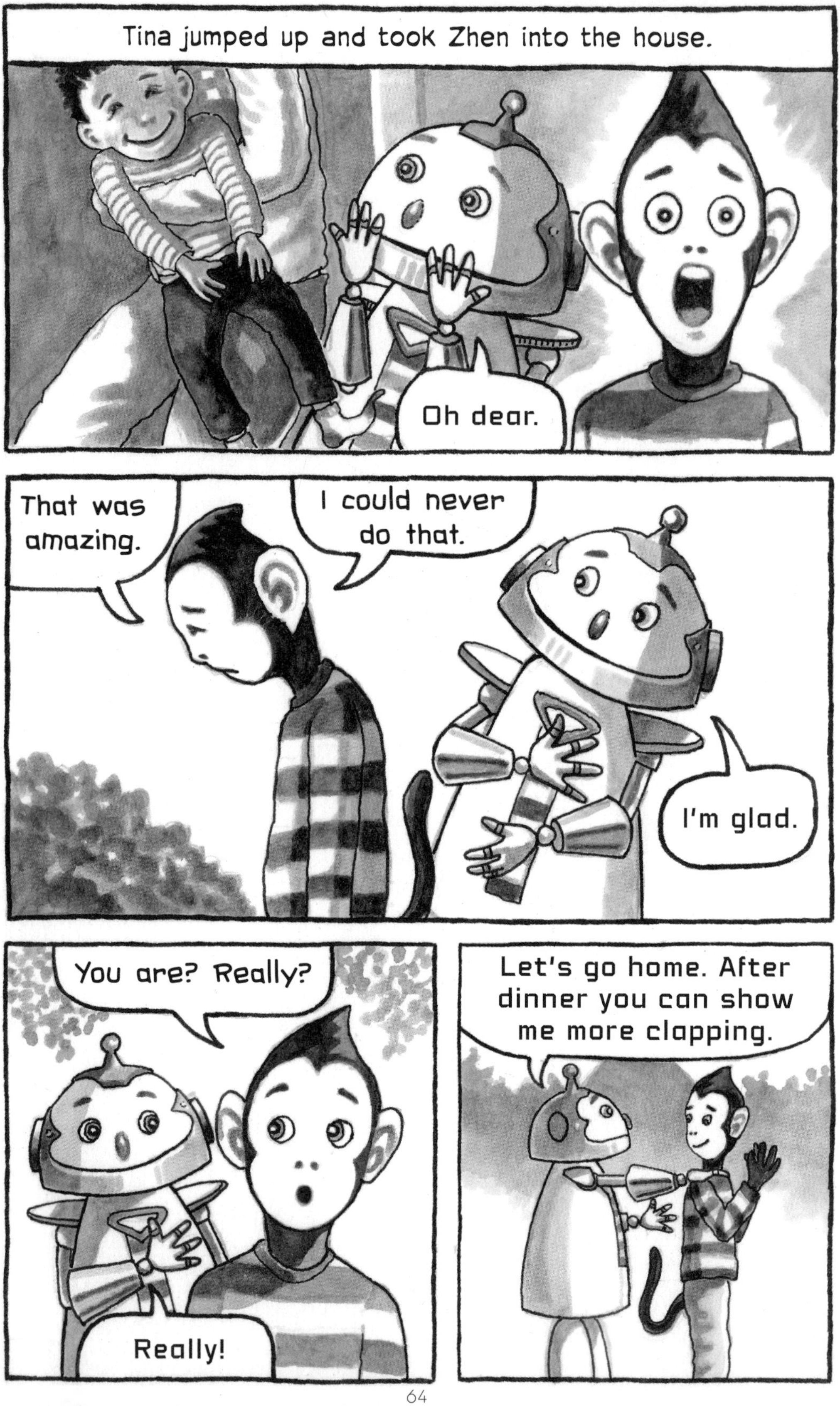

Tina jumped up and took Zhen into the house.
Oh dear.
That was amazing.
I could never do that.
I'm glad.
You are? Really?
Really!
Let's go home. After dinner you can show me more clapping.

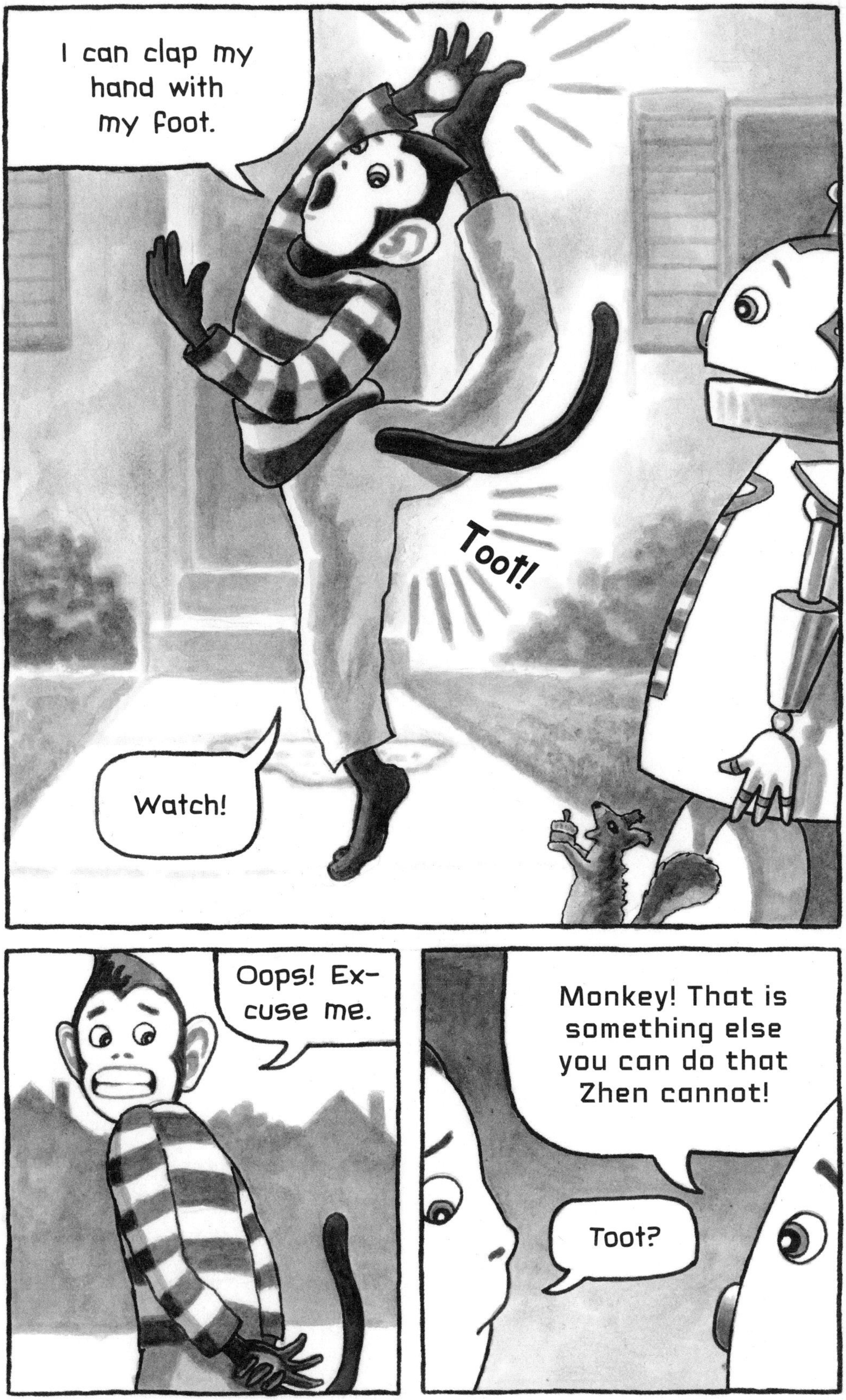
I can clap my hand with my foot.
Watch!
Toot!
Oops! Ex-cuse me.
Monkey! That is something else you can do that Zhen cannot!
Toot?

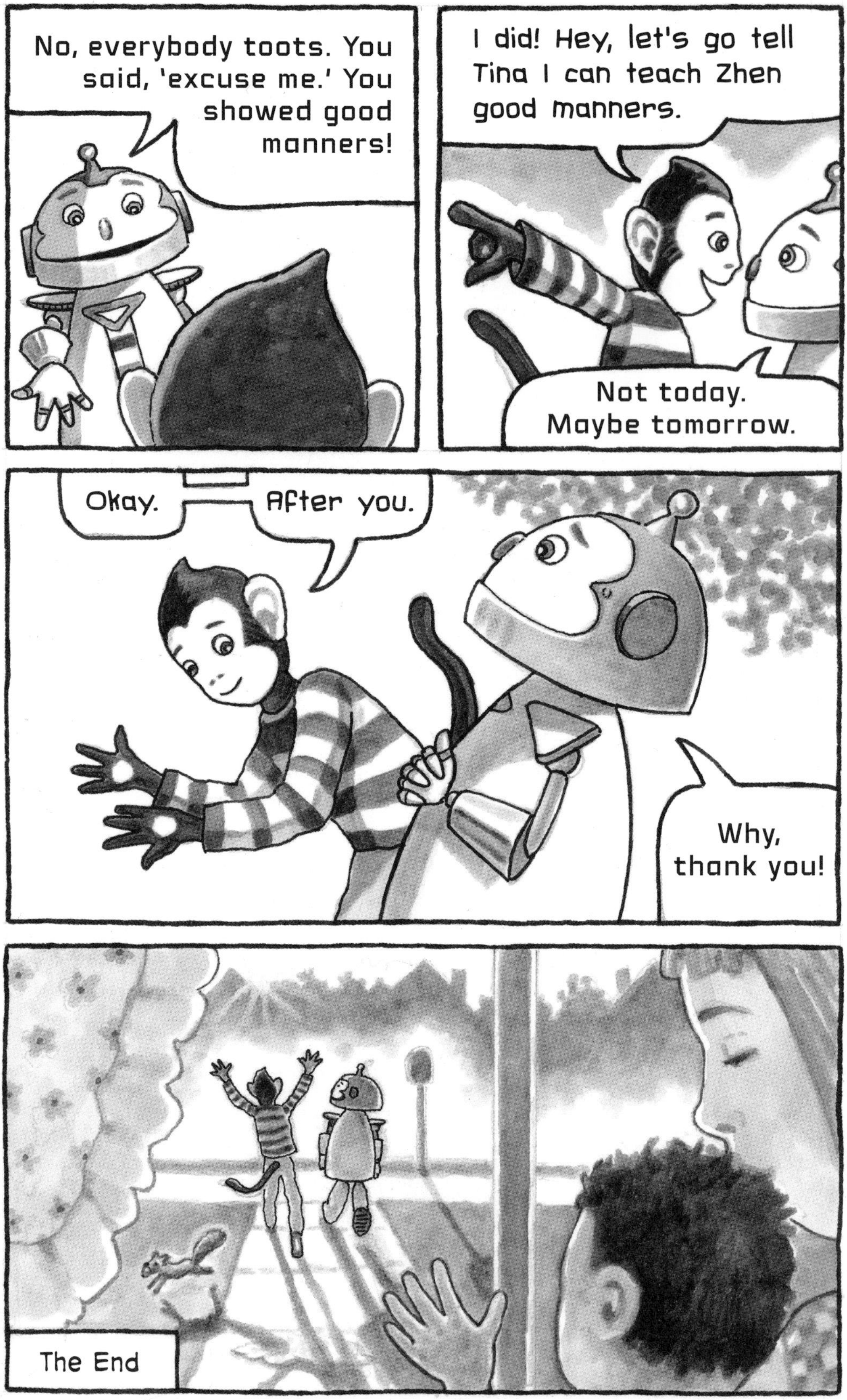
No, everybody toots. You said, 'excuse me.' You showed good manners!
I did! Hey, let's go tell Tina I can teach Zhen good manners.
Not today. Maybe tomorrow.
Okay.
After you.
Why, thank you!
The End

Peter Catalanotto is an award-winning author/illustrator with four dozen books to his credit, including *Monkey & Robot, More of Monkey & Robot, Matthew A.B.C, Emily's Art,* and *Ivan the Terrier.* In 2008 he was commissioned by First Lady Laura Bush to illustrate the White House holiday brochure. Peter also teaches the first children's book writing course offered at Columbia University and Pratt Institute and has visited over 1600 elementary schools in 40 states. Learn more at www.petercatalanotto.com.